Dog Days

MYSTERY
and the
MINISTER'S
WIFE

Dog Days

CAROL COX

GUIDEPOSTS
New York, New York

Dog Days

ISBN-13: 978-0-8249-4800-9

Published by Guideposts
16 East 34th Street
New York, New York 10016
www.guideposts.com

Distributed by Ideals Publications, a division of Guideposts
2636 Elm Hill Pike, Suite 120
Nashville, Tennessee 37214

Library of Congress Cataloging-in-Publication Data.

Cox, Carol.
  Dog days / Carol Cox.
      p. cm.—(Mystery and the minister's wife)
  ISBN 978-0-8249-4800-9
  1. Spouses of clergy—Fiction. 2. Tennessee—Fiction. 3. Dogs—Fiction.
I. Title.
  PS3553.O9148D64 2010
  813'.54--dc22

                                         2009024830

Cover by Lookout Design Group
Interior design by Cris Kossow
Typeset by Nancy Tardi

Printed and bound in the United States of America
10 9 8 7 6 5 4 3 2 1

To Katie,
whose love of dogs
and colorful imagination
inspired some great moments in this story.

Chapter One

What have I gotten myself into?

Forcing her lips into a polite smile, Kate Hanlon shifted slightly in her seat and gazed around the second-floor meeting room of the Copper Mill Public Library with a growing sense of dismay. From the moment Renee Lambert requested—no, demanded—Kate's help with the Harrington County Dog Show, only a month away, Kate suspected she would be out of her depth. Now, given a first glimpse at one of the dog club's meetings, she felt sure of it.

The air inside the meeting room on this Saturday morning seemed to crackle with tension as the dozen or so members of the Harrington County Dog Club reported on the status of show preparations with almost military precision.

Arrangements were being finalized, from securing the transportation and housing of the judges to repairing or replacing any damaged show equipment to obtaining the necessary permits for the show to take place in Copper

Mill Park, which stretched between Main Street and Hamilton Road.

Kate tried to take it all in, hoping she didn't appear as lost as she felt. Between reports, she leaned over and whispered to Renee, who was seated beside her. "Are you sure you want me to help out? I don't have the slightest idea how to run a dog show."

Renee waved her hand dismissively, and the polish on her French-manicured nails caught the light. "That doesn't matter. The thing to remember is that you'll be doing a service to the community."

Kate tried to fight the uneasiness she'd been feeling ever since Renee informed her that she planned to "volunteer" Kate for dog-show duty. She knew she needed to rid herself of the tendency to suspect Renee of having an ulterior motive every time she drafted Kate into some new activity.

And Renee did have a point about this being a way to serve the community. Kate's husband, Paul, had recently wrapped up a powerful series of sermons on ministry by challenging every member of the Faith Briar congregation to develop relationships beyond their church community.

"Don't be afraid to think outside the box," he'd said. "It's time to try some new ideas. If we open ourselves up to what the Lord is saying to us, we'll discover ways of reaching out that we never dreamed of before."

Like helping to run a dog show. Kate's lips twisted in a wry smile. It definitely qualified as something she'd never pictured herself doing.

Renee lifted a soft white-leather tote from the seat on her opposite side and cradled it in her lap. She opened the zippered mesh top and reached inside for Kisses, her beloved Chihuahua. She nuzzled the top of the dog's tiny head with her cheek and murmured, "How's my Little Umpkins? Are you enjoying your brand-new bag?"

The action earned her a reproving glance from Wilbur Dodson, the club president, who was seated at the front table with two other officers. Renee appeared not to notice.

Kate smothered a grin. In the time she and Paul had lived in Copper Mill, she had become used to Renee's insistence on taking Kisses with her wherever she went, and to the loving care Renee lavished on him. Take the new doggie tote, for instance. Apart from the mesh panels on the top and sides, it looked more like a designer hand-bag than a dog carrier. And it probably cost as much, Kate assumed. Renee wasn't one to stint on expense when it came to Kisses and his comfort.

Kate turned her attention back to the meeting and tried not to flinch when she realized the gazes of all three people at the front table were focused on her and Renee.

"Don't let Wilbur intimidate you," Renee huffed in Kate's ear. "He may have produced a champion line of German shorthairs, but that doesn't give him any special privileges."

Kate leaned slightly to her left, hoping to discourage Renee from any more whispering. She should have known better.

"He only beat out Velma Hopkins for club president by two votes in the last election," Renee continued. "Not nearly the landslide victory he'd like to claim it was. Velma wasn't any too happy about having to settle for being vice president."

Kate could believe that. The sharp-faced woman sitting next to Wilbur had propped one elbow on the table and was eyeing Kate with an assessing stare she found unnerving.

At the other end of the table, Lucy Mae Briddle, the club secretary and wife of Copper Mill's mayor, was taking notes.

Renee returned the tote to the empty chair beside her, then leaned closer to Kate. "Velma is determined for her dog to do better at the show than Wilbur's. And she just might get her wish. Her Irish setter has been winning a lot of prizes lately."

Kate smiled politely but didn't offer a comment. She clasped her hands in her lap and willed herself not to squirm under Velma Hopkins' scrutiny. She wasn't used to feeling so out of place, but she supposed this was part of what Paul meant when he spoke about moving outside one's comfort zone.

This meeting was definitely outside hers. Kate thought wistfully about Abby Pippins' request a couple of weeks ago for Kate to lead the Friendship Club, which Abby and Phoebe West were starting.

"Its purpose is to help women find friends and fellowship," Abby had explained. "With your experience as a pastor's wife, you'd be perfect for the job."

"I'll come to as many meetings as I can," Kate had promised Abby, "but God put the idea in your hearts, and I think you and Phoebe are the right ones to head it up."

As much as Kate appreciated Abby and Phoebe for thinking of her for the job, she felt a need to take on a more challenging project that would stretch her the way Paul had been talking about.

And by the look of things, Kate seemed to have found one.

Wilbur Dodson cleared his throat. "We have one more item on the agenda today. We need to fill—"

"'Scuse me. I got something I want to ask."

Kate twisted around in her chair and recognized Bud Barkley, a Copper Mill resident, standing at the back of the room.

"What's he doing here?" Renee murmured. "He isn't a member of the club, and neither are those people with him."

Kate turned back around to see Wilbur glaring at Bud.

"This is a business meeting, Bud," he said. "You can't just jump in whenever you feel like it."

Velma pursed her lips and nodded. "We have to follow the agenda. Parliamentary procedure, you know."

Bud held his ground and hooked his thumbs around the straps of his overalls. "Don't get all riled up, folks. It's just a question. It won't take more than a second to give me an answer."

Wilbur rapped his knuckles on the table. "You're out of order. The chair hasn't recognized you."

Bud snorted. "What're you talkin' about, Wilbur? I've known you ever since fourth grade, when we used to whip the Pine Ridge team at Little League. If you can't recognize me from across the room, you'd better get yourself some new glasses."

Appreciative chuckles circulated among the group gathered near Bud.

Lucy Mae looked at Wilbur with a worried frown. "Should I put all this in the minutes?" she asked in a whisper loud enough for Kate to hear.

Wilbur waved his hand at Lucy Mae and kept his attention focused on Bud Barkley. "You'll need to wait until you're called on to speak, Bud. You're not even part of this club, but if you sit calmly and wait your turn, I'll grant you the floor at the end of the meeting so you can ask your question."

Kate had to give Wilbur credit for digging in his heels. Stocky Bud Barkley was muscular enough to intimidate a man his own size, let alone a weedy specimen like the club president.

Bud looked around at his companions and grinned. "Seein' as how I already have the floor, I think I'll just go ahead and say what I came here to say right now."

The sputtering from the trio at the front table was drowned out by the boisterous approval of Bud's supporters.

Wilbur rose and pounded the table with his fist. "That's enough!" he cried. "This meeting is going to come to order *now*." He glared at the noisemakers until things quieted down.

Bud stuffed his hands in his pockets and rocked back on his heels. "All I want is to ask a question, Wilbur. It's a question I know is on the minds of a lot of other people as well."

He nodded at the group near him, then turned his attention back to the club officers. "We're real pleased that you're gonna hold your dog show here in Copper Mill. But we want to know whether it's gonna be open to real dogs."

A puzzled silence greeted his question. Kate, now sitting sideways in her chair so she could watch all the players at once, glanced at the front table, where all three of the club officers sat with their mouths hanging open.

Wilbur pinched the bridge of his nose between his thumb and forefinger, reminding Kate of a character from a TV commercial for a headache remedy.

He closed his eyes for a moment, then glared at Bud. "What kind of question is that? Of course the show is for real dogs. What do you think we'd be exhibiting, stuffed animals?"

A sprinkling of laughter rippled around the room, and Wilbur looked pleased with himself. He sat up straighter, and a smile stretched across his thin lips.

Bud glowered at him. "That isn't what I mean. What we're askin' is whether this competition is limited to prissy little fur balls, or if it's open to real dogs who can trail a rabbit or tree a possum."

"Or run off a burglar," called the man next to him.

"Or be your kid's best friend," added a red-haired woman.

"That's about the size of it." Bud nodded toward the officers. "Which is it?"

Kate's interest sparked at the idea of the dog show being open to include all the canine residents of Harrington County. At the same time, her heart went out to Wilbur Dodson, whose consternation was evident. If she'd had a bottle of aspirin in her handbag, she would have offered it to him.

But then she caught sight of the expressions on Velma's and Lucy Mae's faces and realized she would have had to extend the aspirin to them as well. When Kate looked at Renee, her concern turned to thoughts of self-preservation as the older woman sprang to her feet and whirled around. Kate ducked to one side just in time to avoid being elbowed in the eye.

Renee quieted the boisterous visitors with a cold stare. "This dog show is intended for pedigreed animals. I hardly see how any other type of canine would qualify."

Bud's face flushed. He opened his mouth, but before he could voice a retort, Wilbur rapped on the table again.

"That's enough! We've listened to your request, and it has been duly noted. Moving on." Wilbur continued as if the interruption had never occurred. "We need to fill Eddie Voight's position. He's been called away to attend to a family emergency in North Carolina and won't be able to help out with the show. Renee Lambert has something to say to us in regard to that."

Renee rose with Kisses in her arms and smiled at her fellow club members. "I do indeed. Eddie's sudden departure has left us in dire need of someone to replace him as head of the hospitality committee."

Hospitality! Why hadn't Renee made that clear to her? Kate sat up straight, feeling confident for the first time since the meeting began. If she had learned one thing after nearly thirty years of being a minister's wife, it was how to be a good hostess and make people feel welcome.

She pressed her lips together to hold back a relieved laugh. The sum total of her knowledge of dogs could be placed in a thimble, but when it came to showing hospitality, she could do it blindfolded. Doing it in a completely unfamiliar setting would probably still prove to be plenty of a stretch for her. She pulled her attention back to what Renee was saying.

"—a heart for serving others, and many years' experience in hosting events of one kind or another. As many of you know, she was a driving force in setting up the Faith Freezer Program at Faith Briar Church. After an undertaking of that magnitude, I believe we can all see that she is more than capable of managing the hospitality aspects of our show."

Renee turned and swept her arm out in a dramatic gesture. "Ladies and gentlemen, I present to you the new head of the hospitality committee for the Harrington County Dog Show—Kate Hanlon."

The burst of applause that greeted Renee's effusive introduction made Kate blush.

"With approval from the membership," Wilbur reminded Renee sternly, then called the meeting back to order.

Kate fought back a chuckle. Given Wilbur's apparent obsession with power, she wondered if he harbored secret political aspirations.

"Mrs. Hanlon has been presented as a candidate for the position of the head of the hospitality committee. Do I hear a motion to accept her?"

Renee resumed her seat and lifted her head regally. "I so move."

"I'll second," called Lucy Mae.

"We have a motion and a second." Wilbur spoke the words almost before Lucy Mae finished, as if he didn't want to lose momentum now that the meeting was finally making headway. "Is there any discussion?"

Kate took a quick breath and raised her hand. Wilbur's eyebrows shot upward, but he nodded in her direction.

"Yes, Mrs. Hanlon. Did you want to say something?"

Kate smiled and stood, turning so she could look at both the head table and the audience.

"Before you cast your votes, I just want to make sure y'all understand that my knowledge of dogs and dog shows is rather limited. To be perfectly honest, my husband and I have never even owned a pet, except for a desert tortoise our kids had when they were little. I'll be glad to help in any way I can, but I don't want you to feel I've come to you under false pretenses."

Wilbur pinched his lips together. "In that case, I'm not sure—"

Lucy Mae leaned forward and beamed. "Wait a minute, Wilbur. That's actually a good thing."

Wilbur's face twisted into a mask of bewilderment, and Lucy Mae chuckled.

"She doesn't have a dog entered in the show," she explained, "so she won't be distracted by grooming or training or other preparations. She'll be free to concentrate on the show itself, and that's a huge plus in my eyes."

Velma Hopkins nodded thoughtfully. "That makes sense to me."

Wilbur blinked, then tapped on the table with his knuckles to get everyone's attention. "Apparently the majority of the officers are convinced. If there is no further discussion, all in favor say aye."

"Aye!" chorused the members.

"Any opposed say nay."

Wilbur slapped the palm of his right hand on the table. "The ayes have it. Mrs. Hanlon, you are hereby elected the head of the hospitality committee for the Harrington County Dog Show. There being no further business, this meeting is adjourned." He whacked the table for the final time.

Rubbing his hand, he leaned toward Lucy Mae and whispered, "Be sure to add another item to the next agenda. This club needs to buy a gavel."

Kate stayed in her seat while Bud and his supporters filed out. When Renee tucked Kisses back into his white-leather tote and headed toward the front of the room, where the other club members were chatting, Kate joined her. She welcomed the chance to get to know these people better and find out more about her new duties.

"Y'all are coming to the workshop on Tuesday evening, aren't you?" Velma asked the group at large.

"Workshop?" Kate murmured to Renee.

"It's put on by the Tennessee Dog Fanciers Association," Renee said. "Top breeders give tips on preparing your dog for the show ring."

Wilbur Dodson folded his copy of the agenda and slipped it into his pocket. "All the clinics in the world won't help someone turn a sow's ear into a silk purse."

Velma stood ramrod straight. "Are you implying that Lord Faernon O'Dale isn't championship quality? I'll have you know—"

Wilbur cut her off with a wave of his hand. "I didn't say that. I'm merely stating that a dog either has what it takes to be a champion or he doesn't."

Kate didn't miss the smirk that accompanied these words.

Neither did Velma. "Spout all you want, Wilbur Dodson. When all is said and done, we'll see who's standin' in the winner's circle on show day."

"I'm in charge of setting up the show equipment." Lucy Mae smiled sweetly. "I'll make sure there's a platform tall enough for Sir Percival to be seen by all the onlookers. Miniature dachshunds are always crowd pleasers."

Velma and Wilbur burst forth at the same time.

"Well, I never—"

"You can't seriously believe—"

Renee cleared her throat. "I don't know what you're all in such a tizzy about."

Her calm remark brought their bickering to a stop more effectively than if she'd shouted.

Lucy Mae gaped at her. "What are you talkin' about? You aren't tryin' to tell us you aren't just as excited as we are to see who wins, are you?"

Renee gave them all a pitying look. "But there isn't any need for you to get all hot and bothered when it's perfectly obvious who's going to take home the Best in Show trophy."

Lucy Mae narrowed her eyes. "And who might that be?"

Renee lifted her doggie tote and inclined her head ever so slightly. "Why, my Little Umpkins, of course."

The room fell silent. Kate shivered. If this moment had been taken from a scene in an Agatha Christie mystery, she'd have known immediately which character would be slated to play the murder victim.

Renee seemed oblivious to the frosty silence that greeted her remark. She smiled as she ran the tips of her fingers across the soft leather tote.

"In fact, I bought this new tote as a gift for Kisses, to celebrate his victory ahead of time."

Velma gasped. Wilbur grunted. Lucy Mae's face turned a light shade of mauve.

Kate sent up a quick prayer for everyone's blood pressure and tugged at Renee's elbow. "I think it's time to leave."

Renee's gaze remained fixed on her competition. "What for?"

Kate decided to leave Renee to her own devices. Smiling, she said, "Well, I have an appointment, so I have to run. It was nice meeting you folks. I'll see you later, Renee."

Renee waved her away, and Kate pushed open the meeting-room door, grateful to escape. As she hurried toward the stairs, she could hear the murmur of heated conversation.

Chapter Two

As Kate made her way to the library exit, she spotted her best friend Livvy Jenner loading books onto a shelving cart and walked over to her. Letting out an exaggerated groan, Kate said, "Why didn't anybody warn me about this?"

The corners of Livvy's eyes crinkled when she laughed. "Was it really that bad?"

Kate rested her elbows on the circulation desk and rolled her shoulders, hoping to loosen some of the tension in her muscles.

"Well, there's good news and bad news. The good news is the job won't be as difficult as I thought. They only want me to head up the hospitality committee, so that shouldn't be a problem."

Livvy set the last book in its place and joined Kate. "So what's the bad news?"

Kate moaned and rubbed her temples. "I had no idea how high emotions can run over a simple pet show."

"*Dog* show," Livvy corrected. "And there's nothing simple about it. There's a fair amount of status attached to a win. Among the dog owners, at least."

The sound of loud, strident voices filtered down from the second floor.

Livvy looked toward the stairwell and grimaced. "It sounds like the party's over."

Some of the patrons in the reading area glanced her way and frowned.

Livvy sighed. "Time to put on my head-librarian hat and remind them that this is a quiet zone. Would it help to talk some more when I get back?"

Kate shook her head. "I already told Renee I have an appointment. I need to be gone by the time they get down here."

"That's right. I forgot you're getting your hair done. Think you'll be finished by noon?"

"I expect to be. Betty's only doing a cut and style today."

"Do you want me to meet you there? We can walk out to your house on my lunch break."

Kate glanced out the library's front window. "I know we need the exercise, but it's so hot and muggy today. Do you mind if we skip the walk?"

"No problem. How about if we drive out to your place instead? It'll give us time to talk, and we can make some fruit smoothies. Will Paul be coming home for lunch?"

"No, he'll be busy all day with the car-care clinic he and Carl Wilson are running this summer. Let's plan on those smoothies. Just the thought of them makes me feel more refreshed."

Livvy grinned. "It's a deal."

When the voices upstairs grew louder, Kate gave Livvy a good-bye wave, then headed out the door. "See you at noon."

The moment Kate felt the warm, moist air wrapping its fingers around her, she was tempted to turn around and retreat back into the cool shelter of the library. But that would have meant running straight into the bickering dog-club members.

She checked her watch. She still had some time to kill before her appointment at Betty's Beauty Parlor. Kate looked eastward and brightened when she saw Sam Gorman's Mercantile across the street. She could stop in there first before heading to Betty's, just two stores down from the Mercantile. It was always fun to browse the shelves in Sam's store to see what new items he might have stocked.

Kate quickly crossed the street to put a little distance between her and the library, then she slowed to a more leisurely pace as she climbed the Mercantile steps and entered the store. There was no need to hurry, especially not in this heat.

"Mornin', Kate," Sam called down from a ladder, where he was busy restocking canned vegetables. "Are you looking for anything in particular?"

"No, just browsing."

"Well, holler if you need help."

Sam went back to stacking cans, and Kate meandered along the aisles, then over to the magazine rack. She flipped through an issue on garden landscaping but found the thought of all that digging in the summer heat too oppressive to contemplate.

Bending over to put the issue back in its place, she spotted another magazine with a large photo of a golden retriever on the cover.

Kate picked it up and thumbed through the pages, her interest mounting when she noted several articles on regional show results. This was just what she needed to help her learn more about her new venture.

She closed the magazine and tucked it under her arm, then she grabbed a cooking magazine with a pull-out section of cookie recipes and headed for the register.

After making her purchase, she stepped outside again. She still had fifteen minutes to go before her hair appointment. The walk to Betty's wouldn't take more than a couple of minutes, even if she dawdled.

Oh well, it wouldn't be a problem to get to the beauty shop a little early. She could sit and read while she waited, and at least Betty had air-conditioning.

She cast a lingering glance inside Emma's Ice Cream Shop when she walked past. A creamy cone would go a long way toward alleviating the daunting heat, but she couldn't afford the extra calories if she wasn't going to burn them off walking with Livvy.

Feeling more than ready to sit down and relax, Kate entered the beauty shop and was greeted by a rush of cool air mingled with the scent of perm solution. After the stress of the dog-show meeting and the altercation that followed, she was looking forward to a bit of pampering.

Her enthusiasm faded a bit when she spotted Lucy Mae Briddle in one of the salon's salmon-colored vinyl chairs.

Lucy Mae's hair was wet, and Ronda, one of Betty's stylists, was getting ready to put it up on rollers. Lucy Mae must have headed there straight from the library, Kate decided.

Elma Swanson occupied the chair at Betty's station, admiring her newly styled hair in the mirror.

"Hi, Kate," Betty called. "You can head on back to the shampoo area. I'll be with you as soon as I set up Elma's next appointment."

While Betty and Elma walked over to the counter, Kate set her handbag and magazines on a shelf under the mirror at Betty's station. Then she headed to the shampoo room at the back of the shop and settled into one of the black vinyl reclining chairs.

Betty joined her a moment later and spread a cape around Kate's shoulders, then tilted the chair back. Kate closed her eyes and let herself relax, enjoying the gentle pressure of the water pulsing through her hair and Betty's nimble fingers massaging her scalp.

"What are we doing to your hair today, Kate? Want to try something different this time?"

"Thanks, but I think I'll just stick with the usual."

Kate knew how Betty loved to experiment with new

hairstyles, but Kate wasn't in the mood for taking chances today. She sat up so Betty could towel her hair dry, then she followed Betty back into the main part of the salon.

As she neared her chair at Betty's station, Kate heard her cell phone ring.

"Oops, just a minute." She offered Betty an apologetic grin and reached for her handbag. After fishing around for a moment, she found the phone and pressed the TALK button. "Hello?"

An unfamiliar voice sounded over the line. "Vera, is that you?"

"Vera? No, you must have—"

"Your voice sounds funny. Do you have one of those summer colds?"

"No, this isn't Vera's phone. You must have—"

"Guess I got a wrong number." The unknown caller disconnected without further comment.

"Sorry about that," Kate told Betty, then she reached over to place her handbag back on the shelf. But as she did, her new magazines spilled out of the shopping bag onto the floor.

"Well, look at that!" Lucy Mae cried, pointing to the dog magazine. "Our new hospitality-committee chairperson is turning into a dog lover already."

"Just want to get up to speed on what to expect," Kate replied with a smile. "The show is only four weeks away. That isn't very long for a total novice like me to get some idea of what will be going on."

She placed the magazines back in the bag and

returned them to the shelf with her purse before taking her seat. Then she set her cell phone to silent mode and tucked it out of sight under the cape as Betty began combing out her hair.

"What show are you talking about?" Ronda asked.

"It's put on every year by the Harrington County Dog Club," Lucy Mae explained. "I'm the club secretary, you know," she added with a modest smile. "This year the show is being held right here in Copper Mill. Be sure to mark your calendar. It's going to be a marvelous event, and you don't want to miss it."

"Cool," Ronda said. "I didn't even know you owned a dog."

"Of course she does." Betty finished combing through Kate's hair and started inserting rollers with practiced ease. "One of those little wiener dogs, isn't it?"

Lucy Mae shot a withering look at Betty. "Sir Percival is a registered miniature dachshund with numerous champions in his pedigree." She pushed herself straighter in her chair and lifted her chin. "He will be a champion in his own right very soon."

Betty reached for another roller. "Must take a lot of work to get a dog ready for something like that."

"Oh, it does. You wouldn't believe how much of my time is devoted to overseeing Sir Percival's diet and grooming and exercise. The list goes on and on."

Lucy Mae heaved a dramatic sigh. "It's a full-time job, and it's all we seem to talk about around the house these days." She gave a little laugh. "Lawton says he's looking

forward to the day when all of this will be over. But I can't
get enough of it."

Betty turned Kate's chair a bit to the right, then said in
a teasing tone, "I don't know. Seems to me you're going to
a lot of trouble for nothing."

Lucy Mae's eyes bulged. "What do you mean?"

"I thought Renee Lambert's Chihuahua was going to
take the big prize this year. The way I hear it, it's practically a done deal already."

"What are you talking about?" Lucy Mae sputtered
like a teakettle coming to a boil. "Whatever put that
ridiculous notion in your head?"

Betty grinned. "Renee was here just yesterday getting
her nails done. She was showing off that new leather doggie tote and telling everyone how Kisses is going to take
home the grand prize."

"That woman!" Lucy Mae erupted. "I've had enough
of her swanking around with that new bag as though that
dog of hers is some kind of celebrity."

She crossed her arms and snorted. "Honestly, it was
disgusting the way she carried on after the meeting this
morning, wasn't it, Kate?"

Kate shifted in her seat and looked at Lucy Mae. She
could think of no socially acceptable way to answer without getting sucked into the beauty-shop gossip for which
Betty and a number of her clients were known around
town. So Kate shrugged and kept silent. Apparently Lucy
Mae decided to press on in spite of Kate's refusal to help
her fan the flames of gossip.

"Goodness knows, I cater to Sir Percival's needs, but never in my life have I seen a dog as pampered as that Kisses."

She let out a sharp laugh. "Kisses! What a ridiculous name for a dog. If the poor little thing could talk, he'd probably tell us all how mortified he is with a moniker like that."

Betty and Ronda joined in laughing at her comments. Encouraged by their response, Lucy Mae showed no signs of slowing down.

"And what about those silly outfits she makes him wear? Why just the other day, she even told me she was ordering matching sweaters for the two of them!"

Betty chuckled, then leaned over and peered at Kate's lap. "What's that light glowing underneath your cape?"

"I have no idea." Kate pulled the cape aside and saw that the screen of her cell phone was illuminated, indicating that someone was on the line.

But how could a call have come in without her knowing it? She frowned, then remembered putting the phone on silent mode. She must have inadvertently pushed the Talk button when she shifted in her chair. Chuckling at the coincidence, she picked up the phone and glanced at the Caller ID. Her smile vanished when she saw Renee's name on the display.

Kate's stomach clenched. How long had Renee been on the line, and how much of Lucy Mae's chatter had she heard? She took a deep breath and spoke in a bright, clear tone. "Hello, Renee."

Betty and Ronda ceased laughing immediately, but Lucy Mae carried on, oblivious to Kate's remark.

Kate had the feeling she sometimes experienced in nightmares, when something had gone horribly wrong, and she couldn't do anything to stop it. She cleared her throat and tried again, speaking louder this time. "Hello, *Renee*. Are you there?"

Lucy Mae stopped midsentence, her mouth hanging open. The sight might have been comical if the situation hadn't been so thick with tension.

Kate's relief at putting a halt to Lucy Mae's commentary on Kisses turned to concern when she heard a raspy moan come over the line.

"What is it, Renee? Has something happened to your mother?" Renee's mother was in remarkably good shape for her ninety-some years, but at that age, a health crisis could arise at any time.

"No." Renee's voice shook with sobs. "It's Kisses. He's been . . . dognapped."

"What?" Kate sat bolt upright in her chair. "But I just saw him with you at the meeting."

"It only happened . . . a few minutes ago," Renee wailed. "I need you, Kate. Can you come?"

Kate blinked back tears. Renee was often a drama queen, but Kate recognized the sound of genuine grief when she heard it. "I'll come as soon as I can. I'm at the beauty parlor right now and Betty's got me in curlers, but I'm sure I can be there in thirty minutes. Are you at home?"

"No." Renee's sobs increased. "I'm at ... the park."

"Why don't you—" Kate caught herself before suggesting that Renee come by the beauty parlor. As fragile as
Renee sounded at the moment, she didn't need to be sub-
jected to its gossipy atmosphere. "Can you get home?" Kate
asked. "You need to sit down and try to collect yourself."

"Yes, I can go home. I just ... I'm scared ... and I
didn't know who else to call."

"Renee, I'm glad you called. I'll meet you at your
house just as soon as I can."

SHOULDERS SAGGING, Kate turned her cell phone off and
slumped back into her seat.

The other women stared at her in silence.

Finally Betty asked, "What was that all about?"

Kate shook her head. "Kisses is missing."

Betty and Ronda went back to work, but without their
usual nonstop chatter. Kate sat in silence while Betty continued to roll her hair, wondering if Kisses had really been
dognapped or if Renee was overreacting.

And how much of Lucy Mae's caustic remarks had
Renee heard? Kate glanced over at Lucy Mae, but Lucy
Mae refused to meet her eyes.

Chapter Three

Thirty minutes later, after calling Livvy to cancel their date, Kate had retrieved her black Honda Accord from the library parking lot and was pulling up in front of Renee's house behind Deputy Skip Spencer's black-and-white SUV. Skip greeted her at the door.

"I'm sure glad you're here, Missus Hanlon. I didn't have a problem taking the missing dog report, but I wasn't sure what to do next."

"How's Renee doing?" Kate asked. "She sounded terribly upset over the phone."

Skip raked his fingers through his already-tousled red hair and nodded toward the living room. "She's in there. I think you'd better see for yourself."

Kate stepped into the entry hall and peered into the beautifully decorated living room.

Renee was huddled at one end of the sofa with her face buried in her hands. Her shoulders convulsed with sobs.

Renee's mother, Caroline Beauregard Johnston, sat beside her, patting her daughter on the knee.

"Oh dear," Kate said.

Skip shook his head. "Yeah, it's bad, all right. I was hoping you might be able to calm her down. I can't seem to get through to her. If she doesn't get ahold of herself soon, I think we may need to call her doctor."

"I'll see what I can do." Kate crossed the room briskly and knelt on the floor in front of Renee. Ignoring the protest from her arthritic knee, she wrapped her arms around the distraught woman.

"Renee, I'm so sorry." She felt shivers rippling through Renee's body. "Can you tell me what happened?"

Renee sniffled loudly, then raised her face to look at Kate. It took an effort for Kate not to gasp at the sight of Renee's haggard appearance. Mascara formed dark circles like a raccoon's mask under her eyes and trailed down her cheeks, smeared by the torrent of tears. Normally Renee would never have dreamt of allowing anyone to see her in such a state, which was a strong indication of how deeply Kisses' disappearance had affected her.

Kate reached for a box of tissues sitting on a small table nearby and handed it to Renee. Renee mopped at her face, then took a series of deep breaths. "I still can't believe this is happening," she began in a shaky voice. "When I drove home after the meeting, Mother said she wanted to get out of the house."

Caroline gave her head a sharp nod. "It's been so hot lately, the walls just seem to be closing in on me."

"I decided we would drive to the park," Renee went on. "I wanted to inspect the area where the dog show will be held. So we walked out into the center of the park, and Mother decided she wanted to go off and stroll around on her own." Renee sniffled. "As hot as it is today, I should have known that would be too much exertion for someone her age."

Caroline leveled a scowl at her daughter but let Renee continue without interruption.

Renee didn't seem to notice her mother's pique. "A few minutes later, I heard her cry out and saw that she had fallen over near the creek. It scared me to death! I thought she might have broken her hip again. Kisses was taking a nap in his new doggie tote, so I set him down in the shade of a tree and ran to help her."

Kate nodded and eyed Renee's mother closely. "Are you all right?"

"Oh, I'm fine." The elderly woman waved her hand in a gesture reminiscent of her daughter's.

"She is," Renee agreed. "I think the heat just got to her. I mean, it was getting to me, and I'm in great shape."

Kate nodded but stifled a sigh at Renee's insistence that she wasn't a day over thirty-nine, even though she was actually in her seventies.

Renee continued. "I helped Mother to a park bench and fanned her a bit, and after a little while, she perked right up. I knew I needed to get her back home, so I helped her to the car. Then I went back to pick up Kisses."

Her lower lip quivered. "But when I got there, the tote was missing . . . and Kisses was gone with it."

Kate gasped. "Oh, Renee, that's awful! Are you sure

you looked under the right tree?" She realized her mistake even before Renee pierced her with a withering gaze.

"I looked everywhere—under every tree and all along the street. I thought some youngster might have carried him off, so I checked the children's play area. Nothing. There was no sign of Kisses anywhere."

Renee's voice rose half an octave. "This is the first time I've ever left him alone, and look what happened. I can't believe I could have been so negligent."

"That wasn't negligence," Kate soothed. "You were doing the right thing by helping your mother."

Relief flickered in Renee's eyes for a moment, then faded. "I shouldn't have left him. He depends on me, and I let him down. I know *some people* may think I spoil Kisses, but he means the world to me."

Kate winced. So Renee *had* overheard Lucy Mae's hurtful comments. Her heart melted to see Renee in such distress.

Renee fluttered her fingers and sniffled again. "I feel so helpless, Kate. You know I'm a person who always likes to take action, but I can't think clearly enough right now to know what to do."

"You've already spoken to Skip," Kate said. "So that's good. I can check with the humane society and see if anyone has taken Kisses there."

Renee nodded, as if Kate had just thrown her a lifeline.

Encouraged, Kate cast about for another idea. "How about putting a lost-and-found notice in the *Chronicle*?"

Renee reached for another tissue. "Or a display ad so

it won't get lost in the classifieds. A quarter page at least, maybe larger." Her shoulders shook again. "But the *Chronicle* won't be out until next Thursday. There has to be something more I can do in the meantime."

"Get on the phone and start calling people," Kate urged. "Put the word out that Kisses is missing. And how about making up some flyers? You can post them around town and ask people to help look for him."

Tears pooled along Renee's lower lids and started trickling down her cheeks again, carrying with them new streams of mascara. She leaned forward and clasped Kate's right hand in both of her own.

"I can do all that, but I need your help, too, Kate. I'm sure the deputies will do what they can, but you love Kisses. You're so good at solving mysteries, and this is a matter of life and death. I want you to find my Little Umpkins and bring him home."

Kate shot an apologetic glance at Skip, then slipped her hand from Renee's grasp and patted the older woman's arm. She stood up and pulled a small overstuffed chair closer to the sofa where Renee sat.

That momentary separation threw Renee into another meltdown. She began wailing all over again. "How could I have done such a foolish thing? Leaving my . . . precious Umpkins there . . . all alone. I walked away from him. This is all my fault!"

Renee seemed to be so distraught that she was on the brink of needing medical attention, so Kate took Renee's hands in her own and spoke firmly. "Blaming yourself won't solve anything, Renee. Let's take it slowly, from the beginning, okay?"

Renee blinked at Kate's tone, but her words had the desired effect. Renee freed one hand to reach for a tissue, then dabbed at her eyes.

"What do you want to know?" She sat up straight and squared her shoulders, looking more like herself.

Kate swallowed hard and sent up a quick prayer: *Lord, give me the right words to say.*

"Did you see anyone suspicious around the park?"

Renee gave Kate a baleful glare. "Obviously, I would have mentioned it if I had spotted the perp or seen anything suspicious. Come on, Kate, what kind of a sleuth are you?"

Kate tried to brush off Renee's jab and her irritating use of cop-show lingo. "Indulge me, Renee."

"Fine. I guess there were several cars parked along Hamilton Road near where we were. But it's tourist season, after all. Strangers are milling around all over town. It could have been anyone."

Kate's shoulders sagged. It wasn't going to be easy to solve this mystery.

"All right. I'll look around and see what I can find out. I can't promise I'll be able to locate Kisses, but I'll do my best."

"Then you'll take the case?" Renee's eyes shone with hope.

Kate nodded. *And Lord, I'm going to need all the help I can get.*

THAT EVENING, Kate arranged thin slices of turkey on flour tortillas, then layered lettuce, tomato slices, narrow strips of green pepper, and shredded cheddar on top. After drizzling her homemade ranch dressing over each stack, she rolled the wraps tightly and smiled when she heard Paul's key turn in the front lock. *Perfect timing.*

With a quick glance to assure herself that the place settings on the oak table were in order, she hurried to greet him with a kiss and a hug. "How did your day go?"

"It was great." Paul threw his arms around her and lifted her off the floor, swinging her in a circle before setting her down again.

Kate gazed at him appraisingly and laughed. "You don't look like a man who's spent a long, muggy day changing oil and checking engines. Speaking of which—" She looked down at his hands and eyed them suspiciously. "You didn't leave greasy handprints on my favorite blouse, did you?"

Paul held out his hands, palms up, for her inspection. "You've trained me well. I was wearing coveralls to keep my clothes clean, and I used some of that waterless hand cleaner before I left Carl's house and got most of it off there. I figured I'd finish up the job here before supper."

"Then you'd better get crackin'. I'm just getting ready to put food on the table."

While Paul washed up in the master bathroom, Kate slid the turkey-ranch wraps onto two dinner plates and carried them to the table, where a freshly tossed salad and a chilled bowl of marinated green beans were already waiting.

Paul returned just as she was setting tall, frosty glasses

of iced tea, garnished with sprigs of mint, beside their plates.

He sat down and rubbed his hands together. "Ah, a fitting reward for a good day's work."

They joined hands and bowed their heads while Paul said grace. After his "Amen," Kate shook out her napkin and laid it across her lap, then she reached for the salad tongs while Paul spooned green beans onto his plate.

"You started telling me about your day," she said, "but we got a little sidetracked with the grimy hands issue." She studied his face for a moment. "It must have been wonderful. As hot as it's been, I thought you'd come home worn to a frazzle, but you look positively refreshed."

Paul sliced off a bite-sized piece of his turkey wrap and speared it with his fork. "When Carl talked to Jeff and Eli and they decided to start the clinic, I was thinking what a blessing it would be for both the guys and the folks they would come in contact with. Maybe even for our entire congregation. But I never thought I'd end up being so blessed myself."

Kate added green beans to her own plate, then drizzled a vinaigrette dressing over her salad. "This is the third time you've held the clinic this summer, but I've never seen you look this buoyant before."

"I think we're beginning to hit our stride. Not only are we working together as a team, but I got to talk to a lot of people about the Lord today. It's a whole different way of ministering to the community than preaching on Sunday or meeting with people in my office at the church."

"That's great, hon. Is the rest of the team enjoying it as much as you are?"

Paul nodded as he took a sip of iced tea. "Carl's feeling really proud about coordinating all the details. Eli didn't know all that much about cars to begin with, but he's learning a lot, and I know he's praying for the needs of the people we're helping."

He paused as he slid a forkful of salad into his mouth. "And then there's Jeff Turner."

Kate smiled at the mention of the thirtysomething young man who had become a regular at Faith Briar over the past few weeks. She finished chewing a bite of turkey and swallowed before she spoke. "He seems very nice."

"He is. Jeff impresses me as a man of good character. I'd like to have him over for dinner sometime so we can both get to know him better. We've talked a bit about his spiritual growth. He's really interested in reaching out to others as well as developing a deeper walk with the Lord. Maybe working with him at the car clinic will give me a chance to do some discipleship training in addition to community outreach."

Paul's voice sounded more excited as he talked. "And the best part is that while we're working on cars, our hands are busy, but we're also talking, and the car owners are listening and even joining in from time to time."

Paul's smile could have lit up the house all by itself. "It's a win-win situation. And it looks like we're going to be able to do this on a regular basis all through the summer. We figure twice a month will give us a good chance to reach out to the community without being inundated with too many jobs at once. If we keep that up, we ought to have all the vehicles in good shape before the cold weather hits this fall."

Kate grinned. "You're turning into quite the mechanic, aren't you? What kinds of repairs did you do today?"

"For the most part, it was pretty routine stuff—changing oil, checking the air pressure in tires, things like that. We installed a new set of windshield wipers on Enid Philpott's car." He snapped his fingers. "Oh, and Lisa Phillips was there with that ancient rattletrap Ford Tempo of hers."

"Hasn't she been there once or twice already?"

Paul chuckled. "She's becoming a regular customer. Last time it was a transmission filter. Today she needed a new radiator hose. It seems like as soon as we get one thing taken care of, something else breaks down. That car is pretty much held together by—"

"Let me guess. Duct tape?"

Paul laughed. "No, although I must admit it's tempting. That thing looks like it's ready to fall apart at any moment. I was going to say it's being held together by maintenance and prayer."

Kate folded her napkin beside her plate. "Do you think she knows her car is being held together by prayer?"

Paul nodded. "I've mentioned that we're praying for her, but I get the feeling she's not into prayer or God. She's always pleasant when she talks to me, but I've noticed that if the conversation turns to anything related to the Lord, she shuts down and looks like she's going to bolt."

"I've had the same experience with her," Kate mused. She pushed a bean around her plate with her fork. "Her daughter Brenna is such a sweet girl, and she really seems to be growing spiritually since she's been coming to the youth group. And she seems to have such a good relationship with her mother. It's hard to understand why Lisa seems so closed to spiritual things when her daughter is so open to the Lord."

Paul swallowed the last of his iced tea and pushed his chair back from the table. "I don't understand it either, but there has to be a reason. God knows what it is, though, and he has infinite patience."

He chuckled. "And I have to remind myself of that when I get impatient about seeing results. In the meantime, our part is to keep on praying and showing her the love of Christ."

Kate smiled. "Even if it's by way of a car-care clinic."

Paul winked at her. "That clinic might be the catalyst that God will use to connect Lisa with him, so we'll just keep reaching out to her and see where he leads us."

"Well, now you've heard about my day. Tell me about yours."

Kate gave a rueful laugh. "Oh my, I don't know where to begin."

She rose and started to clear the table. Paul got up and joined her. While he carried the dishes and silverware to the kitchen sink, Kate returned the salad dressing to the refrigerator. Then she stepped over to the sink and began filling it with hot, sudsy water.

Paul leaned against the counter and regarded her with a bemused expression. He quirked one eyebrow. "I take it that this prolonged silence means you didn't have quite as wonderful a day as I did?"

Kate plunged her hands into the dishwater and started scrubbing the dishes. "Sorry, I guess I got lost in my thoughts." She picked at a stubborn bit of lettuce that clung to one of the plates. "It was a strange day, complete with dog-show mania and poorly timed gossip. And to top it all off"—Kate raised her head to look into Paul's eyes— "Kisses has seemingly been dognapped."

Paul's jaw dropped. "Dognapped? What happened?" He picked up a dishtowel and started drying the dishes while Kate filled him in on all the details. With his help, they finished in no time at all.

"Renee asked me to help find Kisses, and I agreed. I'm not sure how successful I'll be, but I felt she needed some hope to hold on to. She was so distraught, but when I promised to help her, she calmed down a little. I'm worried about her, Paul. I'm not sure she realizes how much resentment she created by insisting that Kisses is going to win."

"I can imagine. Renee tends to be pretty obsessive where Kisses is concerned. So what's your plan? Have you already started sleuthing?"

Kate nodded. "After Skip left, I took her back to the park and had her walk through the whole scenario again.

Kisses and the tote were under one of those big trees along the west side of the park, and her mother fell on the opposite end, near the creek. I can see how someone could have made off with that tote without Renee noticing."

Paul nodded thoughtfully. "Especially when she was so distracted by what had happened to Caroline. But it sounds like you've made a good start. I know the case is in good hands." He squeezed Kate's shoulders and gave her a peck on the cheek before heading to his study to go over his sermon notes for the following morning's service.

Kate sighed as she wiped down the kitchen counters with a damp dishcloth. Despite the lack of physical activity that day, she felt totally exhausted.

Chapter Four

On Monday morning, Millie Lovelace, the church secretary, knocked on the door of Paul's office and stepped inside. "Pastor, there's a man here who wants to see you."

Paul put down the commentary he'd been studying. "Who is it?"

"He says his name is Daniel Newcomb. From the looks of him, I'd say he's probably here to ask for a handout."

Paul flinched. Millie hadn't bothered to close the door all the way when she entered, and he felt sure the fellow in the outer office had heard everything she'd said.

"I'll be glad to talk to him. Send him in." He injected all the warmth he could into his voice to counterbalance his secretary's bristly tone.

Instead of welcoming Paul's visitor into the office, Millie lingered in the doorway. "I've stayed longer than usual today, finishing up that letter you wanted me to type. I really should leave for my job at the SuperMart, but do you want me to stay just in case you need me to call the sheriff or something?"

"That won't be necessary, Millie. You can go. Thanks for everything." Paul tried to keep his voice calm as he stepped past her into the outer office and extended his hand to the waiting man.

"Good afternoon. I'm Paul Hanlon. Won't you come in?"

"I'm not asking for a handout," the man stated, confirming Paul's suspicion that he'd heard every word Millie said. "I just wanted to talk to you a little bit." He followed Paul back into his office, giving Millie a wide berth as he passed by.

Paul shut the door behind them. "Why don't you have a seat, Daniel?"

"No thanks." The other man took a stance in the center of the room. "This shouldn't take long."

Paul studied his visitor. He guessed that the slender young man was in his late twenties. His faded blue T-shirt was tucked into a pair of jeans that had seen better days. Their frayed hems matched the equally frayed laces of his battered sneakers.

He was several inches shorter than Paul, and his sandy blond hair straggled down around the neckline of his T-shirt. Obviously, it had been a while since he'd seen a barber.

Paul could tell he certainly hadn't been overeating. His build bordered on being scrawny, though Paul suspected he had more stamina than one would think at first glance.

Daniel glanced back over his shoulder, as though to reassure himself that the door was closed.

"I'm no freeloader. I just wondered if you had any work that needed to be done around the church."

When Paul hesitated, Daniel hastened to add, "Anything. I'm not choosy. I can do any kind of handyman stuff. I can wash windows or mow the grass. I can clean toilets. Anything."

Paul thought back to a recent church workday when Eli Weston and a crew of men from the congregation had taken care of needed repairs while the ladies banded together to clean the interior of the church from ceiling to floor, windows included.

The man standing before Paul showed every indication of needing financial help. Paul felt tempted to pull some cash out of his own pocket, but he respected a man who wanted to work for his wages instead of receiving a handout.

Seeking inspiration, Paul glanced out the window. The warm weather had boosted the grass into a growth spurt. Though not in terrible shape, it was in need of some sprucing up.

Daniel followed Paul's gaze. "Looks like your grass could use a trim. I'm a good hand with a lawn mower, and I don't need one of those fancy riding jobs. I can even push around one of those rotary mowers if need be."

Paul smiled. "That won't be necessary. We have a decent gas-powered model. But you're right. The lawn could use a little help."

He opened the middle drawer of his desk and pulled out the key to the storage shed. "Come on. I'll show you where the mower is, and we'll make sure it has plenty of gas. If you'd still like something to do when you're finished mowing, the flower beds could use some weeding."

The taut lines in Daniel's face relaxed. "Sure, I'd be glad to."

Paul helped Daniel get started, then returned to his office and settled down to continue preparing the following Sunday's sermon. Caught up in his studying, he was only vaguely aware of the mower's steady hum.

He was jotting a note to remind himself of an important point when a light tap sounded on the door. Paul started and glanced at his watch, surprised to see that three hours had gone by. "Come in," he called.

Daniel stepped inside the office. Bits of cut grass decorated the legs of his jeans, and his hands were decidedly grubby, but he stood a little taller than he had when he'd walked in earlier.

Paul pushed back from his desk and stretched his back. "How's it going?"

"I'm finished. I mowed the grass and weeded the flower beds. Then I noticed that some of the shrubs needed trimming. I found some shears in the shed, so I went ahead and tackled those too. I hope you don't mind. They look a lot better now."

Daniel wiped his arm across his forehead. "If you

want, I can also chop down some of that kudzu on the back side of the shed."

Paul smiled. Daniel had spoken the truth; he was no freeloader.

"I think that's plenty for one afternoon." Paul stood and reached for his wallet, then pulled out three twenty-dollar bills and handed them over.

Daniel counted them quickly before shoving them into his pocket. His eyes lit up, and his chest swelled a bit.

"Why don't you sit down and take a load off?" Paul gestured toward the visitor's chair.

Daniel hesitated, then dropped into the seat. "Thanks."

Paul sat back down in his desk chair and studied his guest, trying to decide why a physically capable young man who obviously didn't mind hard work would have to go knocking on doors to find it.

Daniel didn't look like the type who would take the money and spend it on drugs or alcohol. So why was he looking for odd jobs when he gave every appearance of being employable? There was a story behind this, Paul was sure of it.

"Tell me a little about yourself," he invited. "Are you from around here?"

Daniel looked at Paul as if trying to determine how much he should trust him. He shrugged. "I've lived here for about a year. I'm renting a place a few miles outside of town."

"And you don't have a regular job? I know it can be hard to find work in this area."

"Not right now. I was workin' at a lumber mill, but I got fired a week ago."

"Oh? What happened?"

Daniel shifted uncomfortably in his chair. "I don't know why it is, but I can't seem to hold down a job."

"Really?" Paul said. "You certainly seem to be a good worker."

"I am, or at least I try to be. I get started, and everything goes fine for a while. Then the boss tells me to do something, and I don't do it just the way he wants. The next thing I know, I'm out on the street."

"Is that what happened at the lumber mill?"

Daniel looked down at his tattered shoes and nodded. "Yeah. So I've been poundin' the pavement looking for a new job, but like you said, it's hard to get work around here, especially when you don't have any references. And in a little town like this, it seems like everybody has heard about me before I ever go to see them."

He looked up and met Paul's gaze. "I've got a little bit of money left, but between groceries and rent and gas, that's slipping away pretty fast. I figured maybe I could pick up odd jobs until something better comes along. I've been doing every single thing I can to make money. I've got to take care of my family."

Paul lifted his eyebrows. "You have a family?"

The corners of Daniel's mouth twitched. "Yeah. I have a wife, two little kids, and a pup."

Paul blew out a breath of air. "Then you definitely need a steady income."

Daniel knotted his hands. "That's for sure. It just seems like the world is against me. I can go along for two or three months with no problem, and then something happens, and it all blows up in my face. It doesn't matter what I do or how hard I work, something always goes wrong, and I never see it coming." He made a fist and slammed it into the palm of his other hand.

"I can only imagine how difficult it is for you right now." Paul stood up and offered his hand. "I need to get back to work, but I want you to know that I'll be praying for your success in finding a job, and I'm available any time you'd like to talk some more. In the meantime, feel free to come back if you'd like to go after that kudzu."

Daniel smiled and returned Paul's handshake with a firm grip. "Thanks, Pastor. I just may do that."

KATE PUT TWO SMALL STEAKS into a gallon-sized, resealable plastic bag, then poured in a marinade blended from honey, soy sauce, olive oil, and balsamic vinegar. Zipping the bag shut, she placed the package in a glass dish and set it in the refrigerator.

Sighing, she folded her arms and leaned back against the refrigerator door. Here it was, two days after Kisses' disappearance, and the little dog still hadn't been found. Renee told Kate she had spent every waking moment since the dognapping calling everyone she could think of who might have seen Kisses, but to no avail. Kate had assured Renee that she'd already kicked her sleuthing mind into gear as promised, but the visit she and Renee had made to the park on Saturday afternoon hadn't turned up any clues, as she'd hoped it might. She tried to reassure herself that the little dog would be home soon, but she wasn't quite convinced.

Kate glanced at her watch. Two o'clock. Nearly an hour before she had to leave for the first Friendship Club meeting at Abby Pippins' house. Just enough time for her to do some stained-glass work in her studio.

Kate started toward her studio, then hesitated. Working on something creative usually calmed her when she was feeling restless, but her concern for Kisses wouldn't let her concentrate on anything else. She felt the need for physical activity instead.

She snatched up her keys and her purse, then went out to her car.

She pulled out of the driveway and drove south on Smoky Mountain Road, then she made a left turn onto Hamilton. Passing the park, she continued to the point where Copper Mill Creek meandered along the eastern edge of town.

After parking the Accord on a grassy spot under a yellow poplar, she locked her purse in the trunk and pocketed her keys.

Grateful for the pleasant summer breeze that greeted her, Kate set off on the walking path that ran beside the edge of the creek. She needed to spend some time in prayer for Renee and for Kisses' safe return, and this was a perfect place to do it. Being outdoors in God's creation always made her feel especially close to him.

The splash and babble of water rippling over the rocks acted as balm to her soul. But even while she enjoyed the calming sounds of nature, the same thought kept running through her mind: *What happened to Kisses? Has he really been dognapped? If he was taken by mistake, why hasn't he been returned by now?*

The thought of the little dog being in any danger made Kate's stomach tighten into a hard knot. Part of her wanted to press on at a faster pace, as though that would speed up her brain and bring the answers she sought. But even though the weather was a few degrees cooler that afternoon, she still didn't want to arrive on Abby's doorstep a sweaty, bedraggled mess.

Reining in her desire to speed ahead, she settled down to a leisurely pace.

Lord, this doesn't make any sense, she prayed. *How could Kisses just disappear like that? Renee is worried sick, and I can't blame her. Would you somehow guide us to him, please?*

And while I'm on the subject of dogs, Lord, you know how uncomfortable I feel about being involved with the dog show. It is so not me. After seeing that group in action, I'm not sure how being on this committee is supposed to help draw people toward you, but I want to do this for your glory, not mine. You see the big picture, while I can see only a tiny slice of it. Please help me know the best way to handle this.

Kate fell silent and waited for an answer as she continued walking, her shoes making soft brushing sounds against the thick grass that lined the pathway.

Despite her plea for guidance, no answer came. Even so, lifting her concerns up to the Lord made her feel more at peace than she had since agreeing to attend the dog-show meeting with Renee.

She rounded a bend and realized that she was nearing the footbridge that spanned the creek.

Kate looked at her watch and saw that she would need to head back soon. She decided she would stop at the bridge, enjoy the view for a moment, then turn around.

I guess I can't expect to get answers on demand, can I, Lord? I'm just going to have to trust you to provide them at the right time.

She glanced ahead to check her progress toward the bridge, but dense branches of a large serviceberry bush screened it from sight. As she drew closer to the bush, she heard voices.

Kate stopped. The last thing she wanted to do was to intrude on a private conversation. Walking all the way to the bridge was an arbitrary goal anyway. There was no reason she had to continue that far. The rush of the water made it impossible to distinguish the words being spoken, but the tone sounded tense and angry.

A female voice grew louder, almost to a shout, and Kate's concern mounted. Though the bridge wasn't very far from downtown, it was still a bit isolated. She

didn't want to turn away if someone needed help. Nor
did she want to walk into the middle of a dangerous
situation.

Thank goodness for cell phones! At least she would
have a means of summoning aid if the situation warranted
it. Kate reached for her purse, then realized she had left it
locked inside her trunk. Her stomach clenched. So much
for that idea.

She debated a moment longer, then she took a few
steps forward and peered through the serviceberry
branches. Through the screen of glossy leaves, she caught
sight of a slender, dark-haired teenage girl.

Her back was toward Kate, but a moment later, she
turned so that Kate saw a side view and recognized the girl
as Brenna Phillips. From the stormy expression on her
face, Kate felt sure that Brenna was one of the speakers
she'd overheard.

Kate leaned as far as she could to one side but still
couldn't see the person Brenna was talking to. From the
lower timbre of the voice, she felt sure it was male.
Tension gripped her. What was Brenna doing out there on
the bridge, who was she talking to, and why were the two
of them involved in a shouting match?

Kate felt distinctly out of place crouching behind a
bush, eavesdropping. She was just about to head back
when she saw a flash of white plummet from the bridge,
then heard a loud splash as the object fell into the babbling water.

She caught her breath. Had someone fallen over the bridge railing? Or been pushed?

She started forward, praying that Brenna was all right. Then she heard both voices again, in much less strained tones this time.

Brenna stepped back into view, and Kate saw the girl give her companion an easy smile. Then she threw her head back and laughed.

Much relieved, Kate eased back and slipped away unnoticed. She hurried back toward her car, glad she hadn't gone charging like some avenging angel into what was apparently a minor spat between friends.

A few minutes before three o'clock, Kate pulled up in front of Abby's house on Sweetwater Street and parked along the curb. Reaching into her purse, she turned off her cell phone, not wanting to disturb the meeting.

She crossed the neatly tended lawn and rang the bell. A moment later, Abby swung the door open, her pleasant face flushed with excitement. Phoebe West stood behind her, cradling her baby, Violet, in her arms.

"Welcome!" Abby spread her arms wide and enveloped Kate in a warm hug. "You're the first to arrive. We're so glad you're here."

Kate walked through the door and Phoebe reached out to give Kate a one-armed hug. Little Violet looked up at Kate and gurgled.

Kate glanced around the living room and gave a nod of approval. "I like the way you've set things up. The circled chairs and oversized pillows give the room a very cozy, welcoming feel."

Abby beamed. "We decided not to line the chairs up in rows or do anything else to make it seem like a formal gathering. We want people to be able to relax and enjoy being a part of this group. That's what it's all about."

A tiny frown puckered Phoebe's forehead. "We were a little concerned about the meeting time. Do you think three o'clock on Monday afternoons will work all right?"

"We know most of the working women won't be able to come at this hour," Abby put in. "But our first thought was to reach out to stay-at-home mothers and retirees— women who are at home all day and don't have interaction with co-workers or other adults."

"And we knew that if we made it any later," Phoebe added, "the moms who've been taking care of little ones all day will be busy getting supper ready for their husbands and putting the babies to bed."

"I think that makes a lot of sense," Kate said. "Do you have any idea how many will be coming today?"

Abby gestured toward the chairs. "I really don't expect more than eight or ten. I've asked Patricia Harris and several other ladies from church to come, and I've gone up and down the block inviting women I know are home all day."

Phoebe brightened. "That reminds me. I asked Lisa Phillips to come."

Abby clapped her hands. "So did I! She waited on me

at the fabric store in Pine Ridge when I went in to buy some quilt batting last week. I know her schedule varies, so she'll have some Mondays off. Maybe getting two invitations will let her know we really want her to join us."

Phoebe shifted Violet to her other hip and used a terry-cloth bib to wipe a bit of drool off the baby's chin. "It may take a while before she'll finally come. I'm not going to stop inviting her, though."

"Me, neither." Abby folded her arms across her rather ample bosom. "There aren't many people in her life right now, and she needs to know we want to be her friends."

Praise welled up in Kate's heart. If Abby and Phoebe could convey the love and concern they felt for Lisa to everyone in this group, she felt sure that God would bless their efforts.

She started to tell them so, but the doorbell interrupted her. Both hostesses hurried to greet the new arrivals. It appeared that the rest of the women had chosen to arrive at the same time.

Five or six ladies entered the living room chattering like a flock of magpies. Kate knew Patricia Harris; the others were women she'd seen around town but hadn't met.

Phoebe pointed to the punch bowl, which was set on a table off to one side. "Help yourselves, ladies. The punch is icy cold, and I know it will taste good on a warm day like this."

Kate waited in line to fill her glass. The frothy, pink liquid was every bit as refreshing as it looked.

Once the women had settled in their chairs, Abby stepped to the front of the room and cleared her throat. "Welcome to the first meeting of the Friendship Club." She smiled at everyone present. "The name of the club explains its purpose. We want to reach out to women in the community who may not have a close network of friends. Of course," she added with a laugh, "if you already have friends around town, you're still welcome. But our main goal is to reach out and befriend those who may not have any close friendships."

"And who may not even realize how much they need them," Patricia Harris added. "I know firsthand how easy it is to fall into that trap."

Kate smiled and whispered a prayer of thanks. Patricia had come a long way from the dejected person she'd been when Kate first met her. At that time, Patricia had been trying to cope with her daughter's battle with leukemia while still grieving from the loss of her husband. But people had reached out to her in love, and as a result, Patricia's faith had blossomed.

"Phoebe and I would love for this group to expand," Abby went on, "so we encourage you to invite others."

A young woman with short blonde hair raised her hand, then turned to address the rest of the group after Abby gave her an encouraging nod. "I'm one of those people who really need other women in my life. I'm glad you and Phoebe invited me to come here. With three little kids at home, it seems like all my time is consumed with doing things for them. I'd love to ask other people to be a part of this, but how do I do that when I don't know that many women to invite?"

"For those of you who haven't met her yet, this is Stephanie Miller," Abby said. "And that's a very good question. We welcome anyone to this group: friends, family, even acquaintances—people you know but aren't especially close to. Think of the women you come into contact with on a regular basis, like a cashier at a store where you shop."

Stephanie sat up straighter. "Like some of the other moms I see down at the park? Okay, I could do that. I may not know all their names, but I know them well enough to say hi and talk about the weather and our kids. I wouldn't have to make a big deal out of it, just bring the club up in the conversation and invite them to come, right?"

"Absolutely." Abby's head bobbed up and down. "And feel free to invite strangers, people you don't encounter regularly. Maybe even someone you've met for the very first time.

"If you think of yourself as a pebble tossed into a pond with ripples spreading out in concentric circles, you can see how your influence can spread over a broad area.

"All of us spend much of our time in our own homes, but that doesn't mean we can't have an impact on our community . . . and beyond."

Stephanie piped up again. "This is getting really exciting. What's next?"

Abby and Phoebe looked at each other. Kate could see Phoebe give a little shrug.

Abby laughed and said, "This is where we eat refreshments and begin to get to know each other."

Abby and Phoebe disappeared into the kitchen. When they came back, Abby bore a platter of bite-sized vegetables, crackers, and dip, and Phoebe carried a tray of cookies.

After setting them on the table next to the punch, Abby called out, "Enjoy yourselves, ladies, you may just find people here who will become lifelong friends!"

Laughter bubbled around the room as the women got up and moved toward the refreshment table.

Kate stayed only a few minutes longer. With her concern for both Renee and Kisses mounting, she found herself far too distracted to mingle. She would have to get acquainted with the other Friendship Club members at the next meeting. At that moment, she just needed time to think.

Chapter Five

Kate spent a restless night fighting her way through a disturbing dream. It began with a series of villains holding out glittering trophies to try to lure little dogs into their clutches, then it shifted to a nightmare of a shadowy Cruella De Vil chasing Kisses, who was running in the midst of a band of spotted puppies.

Eventually she was jarred awake by a close-up view of Kisses' face, his doleful brown eyes imploring her to come to his rescue.

Kate was thankful that a strong cup of coffee and her morning devotions helped steady her nerves and restore her focus. It seemed she was swept up once again in a mystery. But this mystery was more personal than any of the others she'd been involved in. After all, Kate had taken care of Kisses for several weeks when Renee's mother was recovering from a broken hip shortly after the Hanlons moved to Copper Mill. Renee had even taken to calling Kate "Grandma" after the hours Kate had spent dog sitting. In spite of the undesirable moniker, Kate had grown to care for the tiny pooch. But it was also personal for Kate because as much as Renee rubbed her the wrong way, she cared for her and couldn't bear to see her so devastated.

At the same time, the thought of solving another mystery filled her with excitement. God had given her a unique gift, and she looked forward to another opportunity to help a friend.

Immediately after breakfast, she returned to Copper Mill Park and walked back over every inch of the area she had covered with Renee on Saturday. To her frustration, she still didn't see anything that stuck out as a clue. Kate stood under the trees that lined one edge of the park.

As much as Kate didn't want to believe that Kisses had been abducted, it seemed like the only real possibility. Questions flooded her mind as she surveyed the grassy expanse in front of her. How had the so-called dognapper chosen that particular time and place? It was the one moment Kisses had been left alone, but how would anyone have known to expect that? Was it just a crime of opportunity? What possible motive could someone have had for taking the tiny Chihuahua? Or had the thief only wanted to steal the expensive leather tote, not knowing what was inside? Why hadn't Kisses barked like he usually did when strangers got too close?

Despite the heat of the day, a chill rippled through her as she considered a more sinister possibility. What if

someone had been following Renee with the intent of taking Kisses? Had the dognapper orchestrated Caroline's
fall, knowing it was the only way to separate Renee from
Kisses?

Kate slowly nodded, picturing the way it might have
happened.

The setting was ideal for just such a heist. If the
perpetrator—or *perp*, as Renee liked to say—had been
spotted at the park, what of it? It was the perfect place for
someone to stretch his—or her—legs and get a bit of
exercise.

No one would have suspected what the thief was
really up to. The caper would have been relatively risk-
free, except for the moment when he snatched the bag
and made off with it.

Kate noticed the temperature starting to climb in
earnest with the rising sun. She returned to her car and
drove back to her house. There was nothing more the park
could tell her anyway, at least not at that moment.

When she arrived home, she headed straight for the
kitchen, poured herself a cold glass of iced tea, and sipped
it while returning to a previous avenue of thought. Maybe
considering the reasons *why* someone would have taken
Kisses would help her discover *who* had committed the
crime.

Kate found herself liking the idea. She could emulate
Hercule Poirot, Agatha Christie's famous detective, and
use psychology to identify the culprit.

What would cause someone to do this? Kate pulled a

pad of paper and a pen from the kitchen drawer and prepared to jot down possibilities.

She closed her eyes and thought back over some of
the mysteries she had read. Why did people commit a
crime?

Money was always a likely factor. Greed figured into
many an illegal act. Kate wrote "Money/Greed" at the top
of the page.

What else?

Hatred. Revenge. Kate shuddered. Her thoughts were
running along a path that was entirely too dark.

She went back to the first point on her list: greed.

That didn't make much sense. Kisses meant the world
to Renee, but as far as Kate knew, the little dog wasn't
worth a vast amount of money. It wasn't as if the thief had
purloined a van Gogh that could be sold on the black market for a fortune. She tapped her pen against the paper.

What about hatred? Her mind flashed back to all the
faces glowering at Renee after her confident prediction of
Kisses' "sure win" at the dog show.

Kate remembered her own sense that if the meeting
had been a scene in an Agatha Christie novel, Renee
might well have been slated as the murder victim.

Was it possible? Her stomach tightened. She didn't
want to believe it, but she had witnessed firsthand
the animosity radiating from the other dog owners in
response to Renee's bragging. But was that really motive
enough to push someone to steal a beloved pet?

Kate looked down at her third point: revenge.

Revenge for what? Kisses hadn't actually won the show, at least not yet.

Knowing as little as she did about such things, Kate had no idea how well Kisses would do in this type of competition, but surely there were other dogs who would give the little Chihuahua a run for his money. Lucy Mae's dachshund, with all those champions in his pedigree, sprang to mind.

In that case, it wouldn't be a matter of getting back at Renee for something that had already happened, but of preventing something from happening. And what was the likelihood of that? The members of the Harrington County Dog Club were respected citizens in their communities, not criminals.

None of it made sense, and yet . . .

Kate couldn't shake the feeling that it all came back to the way Renee had carried on after the meeting, when Renee showed off her new doggie tote, telling everyone that it was an early present to celebrate Kisses' upcoming victory.

Memories of Velma's response to Wilbur's silk-purse comment, and Lucy Mae's outrage over Kisses' presumed win flitted through her mind. She never would have guessed the depth of emotion that went along with showing dogs if she hadn't heard those comments firsthand.

Kate continued her musing while she pulled open the refrigerator door and started gathering the ingredients for a light salad.

The phone rang, interrupting her thoughts. Kate

picked up the receiver and smiled when she heard Paul's voice.

"How would you like to go to the Country Diner for lunch?" he asked.

"That sounds perfect. But I'll need you to be a sounding board. My mind is spinning about Kisses' disappearance."

"I wouldn't expect anything else from you, Katie. I'll pick you up in a few minutes."

Kate hung up the phone and returned the salad fixings to the fridge, then she hurried to brush her hair and freshen her lipstick.

As she stood in front of the bedroom mirror, she returned to her musings. Could a member of the dog club be responsible for the crime? Would any dog lover, no matter how irritated by a competitor's attitude, be willing to inflict that kind of pain on another dog owner?

Kate ran pictures of the club members through her mind like scenes from one of Renee's favorite cop shows, trying to envision any of them engaged in this kind of ruthless act. They all appeared to be fine, upstanding citizens, but Kate didn't know them well. It was possible that a darker personality lurked behind one of those upright exteriors.

AT THE DINER, Kate picked at her blackened-chicken salad while she told Paul about her dognapping theories.

When she finished, she looked up at him. "Is there anything I've missed?"

Paul waited until he finished a bite of his tuna melt on

rye before speaking. "It seems like you've covered every-thing as far as I can see." He reached over and squeezed her hand. "I'm sorry, hon. I'd love to help, but sleuthing is your gift, not mine."

Kate tightened her fingers around his. "You may not be a very useful sounding board, but at least you're cute," she teased.

"Y'all want some pie to finish off that meal?"

Kate looked up to find LuAnne Matthews standing at the table, ready to take their order.

The red-haired waitress grinned at Paul. "Apple's on the menu today, and Loretta just pulled a fresh one from the oven."

"Sounds good." Paul rubbed his hands together. Then he flickered a look at Kate and cleared his throat. "But I probably shouldn't."

Kate tried to maintain her stern expression, then gave in. "We could split a piece," she offered.

Paul's eyes lit up. "À la mode?"

"Don't push it," Kate warned.

"LuAnne said it just came out of the oven, and it's a hot day. I was just trying to help us keep cool."

His attempted innocence wouldn't have fooled a child.

Kate laughed and relented. "All right. À la mode."

"Right." LuAnne jotted a note on her pad and gave Paul a broad wink before she went back to the kitchen.

She returned a moment later and set two plates on

their table, each holding narrow slices of decadent-looking apple pie with a dollop of ice cream on top.

"Here, I went ahead and split it for you to make sure they came out even." She cleared her throat and gave Paul a meaningful glance.

"Y'all need anything else?"

When Paul shook his head, LuAnne left the check on the table and turned to greet new customers coming through the door.

"There's an empty table right over here, folks. Come on in and sit down."

Kate glanced up and saw a couple she hadn't seen around Copper Mill before. The tall, rawboned man and frowsy-haired blonde walked past without acknowledging Kate's welcoming smile. Kate made a mental note of the new faces and looked past them to someone she did recognize.

She kept the smile on her face while Mayor Lawton Briddle headed for a nearby table. Lucy Mae trailed after him, followed by a brown-haired teenage boy.

At the sight of Lucy Mae, Kate felt her shoulder muscles tense and made a deliberate effort to relax them. Saturday's events were still fresh in her mind.

To her relief, the Briddles merely smiled and nodded, then busied themselves with their menus.

Kate picked up her fork. Loretta's apple pie was every bit as good as expected, and Kate almost found herself wishing they had each ordered a full-sized slice. Then she thought of her waistline and decided they had made the right choice after all.

She still had a couple of bites to go when Paul finished and walked over to the cash register to pay their bill. He came back and held Kate's chair for her. When they passed the Briddles' table, Lucy Mae looked up and smiled.

"How nice to see you again," she gushed.

"Good to see you too." Paul reached out and shook hands with Mayor Briddle, then with Lucy Mae. Then he extended his hand to the boy.

"I don't believe we've met. I'm Paul Hanlon, the pastor of Faith Briar Church. This is my wife, Kate."

Lucy Mae patted the teen's arm. "This is my nephew, Micah Jamison. He's spending the summer with us."

Micah rose and gripped Paul's hand.

"Nice to meet you," Paul said. "I hope you enjoy your visit."

"Thanks. It's always good to spend time with Aunt Lucy Mae and Uncle Lawton." Micah gave his aunt a broad grin.

Lucy Mae smiled up at him, then shifted her gaze to Kate and tilted her head to one side. "I hear you're looking into the disappearance of Renee Lambert's dog."

The tension in Kate's shoulders returned. She would have preferred more time to devote to her investigation before word got out, but obviously that wasn't going to happen.

Kate nodded and said, "Renee asked me to see if I could learn anything."

Lucy Mae rested her arms on the table and leaned forward. "And have you?"

Kate hedged. "It's still early . . ."

"Well, I certainly hope you get it all settled before our show. We wouldn't want anything to distract you from your duties there."

Lawton rolled his eyes and looked up at Paul. "I'll be a happy man when this show is over. Maybe as mayor I should have lobbied against letting them hold it here. That's all we ever talk about around the house anymore. Percy this, and Percy that. It's enough to—"

"Sir Percival," Lucy Mae corrected him with an austere look.

Micah leaned forward. "But think about it, Uncle Lawton. It will really increase the value of Sir Percival's puppies if he wins."

Lucy Mae reached over to pat Micah's arm again and gave him a fond smile.

"Lawton, you could take some lessons from our nephew. Micah is ready to pitch right in. He's already agreed to help set up the bleachers and run little errands for me."

She turned to Kate with a proud smile. "And Lawton is going to give a welcoming speech to open the festivities. This show will really be a family affair."

Her husband rolled his eyes again.

"Speaking of the show . . ." Lucy Mae hitched her chair closer to where Kate stood. "I thought I'd make a batch of my famous blueberry-apricot muffins as a thank-you gesture for all the work the judges will be putting in on show day. But as an exhibitor, it wouldn't do for me to present them to the judges directly."

"Hardly," Kate agreed. "That might be construed as an attempt at bribery."

"Exactly! But I thought perhaps you could give the muffins to them in your capacity as hospitality chairperson."

"And be sure to mention that they came from you?" Kate asked drily.

Lucy Mae's eyes twinkled, and Kate felt sure she had hit on the whole point of this little exchange.

"Well, if you just happen to let that slip out . . ." Lucy Mae let the words hang in the air.

Kate assumed an innocent expression. "I probably shouldn't do that. I wouldn't want it to come across as an effort to sway their votes and cause them to look at Sir Percival in a negative light."

Lucy Mae sat bolt upright and pressed one hand against the base of her throat. "Oh, I wouldn't want that!"

"I'm sure you wouldn't." Kate eyed Lucy Mae, wondering just how far the woman would go to ensure a win for her precious dachshund. She looked over at Paul. "I suppose we'd better be going."

"Right you are. I need to get back to the church." He smiled at the Briddles. "It was good chatting with the two of you. And it was nice to meet you, Micah. I hope we see you again."

He walked over to the door and held it open for Kate. After they were out on the sidewalk, he whispered, "I can

see what you mean about people being fixated on winning. Are they all like that?"

"No." Kate made a sour face. "Some of them are worse."

Paul shook his head and looked off into the distance.
"It gives a whole new meaning to the term *dog days*,
doesn't it?"

Kate grinned and playfully elbowed him in the side.

As they walked toward Paul's pickup, they saw Deputy
Skip Spencer heading toward them. He appeared to be
checking vehicles for parking violations, "maintaining a
visible presence downtown," as he called it.

"Well, if it isn't the Hanlons," he called when he spotted them. His deep voice seemed a strange contrast to his
boyish appearance.

"Hey, Skip." Paul strolled over to join the twenty-five-
year-old deputy, with Kate at his side.

"Any success on turning up a lead on Kisses?" Kate
asked.

Skip tapped his ticket book against his leg. "We asked
around, but we didn't find anybody who saw anything.
And there's no evidence in the park. Some dog owners
have their animals implanted with a microchip, but Kisses
doesn't have one. At this point, we've done about all we
can."

He planted his hands on his hips and shook his head.
"After all, it isn't like we're talking about a kidnapped
child. It's only a dog."

Kate reached out to pat him on the arm. "It's more than

that, Skip. You have to realize that Kisses is practically Renee's whole world. To her, this is like having her child taken."

Skip rubbed his forehead. "You'd sure think so from the way she's been calling to ask what progress we've made."

Paul chuckled. "That wouldn't explain why you're patrolling outside this afternoon, would it?"

"It's important to maintain a police presence . . ." Skip trailed off and gave him a sheepish grin.

"Well, it does get me away from the desk and the phone. I mean, she's already called my office over a dozen times today, and she's been in touch with Sheriff Roberts at his office up in Pine Ridge as well."

Kate blinked. "She went over your head and contacted the sheriff directly?"

As soon as the words left her lips, she knew how ridiculous her question was. Of course Renee would go straight to the top with her demands for help. Kate's point about Kisses filling the place of a child in Renee's life was right on target. What would she and Paul have done if one of their three children had been abducted?

Kate knew she would have been at least as determined as Renee to make sure no stone was left unturned.

Skip nodded miserably. "She sure did, and he's called me a couple of times himself. He'd really like some results soon, if there's any way to get them." He hiked his duty belt higher on his waist. "The trouble is, I feel like all I'm doing is running into dead ends. I honestly don't know which way to turn next."

He looked at Kate with a haggard expression. "Do you have any idea who might have done it?"

"No, I think you and I are in the same boat. I haven't come up with a thing so far."

"Well, if you think of anything, be sure to let me—" Skip broke off abruptly, his eyes fixed on a point over Kate's shoulder.

His face paled until his freckles stood out in sharp contrast to his fair skin. "Oh no."

Chapter Six

What on earth?

Kate wheeled around and saw Renee Lambert's large pink Oldsmobile approaching. It pulled into a parking space in front of them.

"Oh boy, I'm going to catch it now," Skip muttered, sounding more like a truant schoolboy than a guardian of the law.

Renee emerged from the car and beckoned to Skip with an imperious gesture.

Skip hooked his thumbs in his duty belt and stood his ground.

Renee narrowed her eyes. Her high heels clacked across the sidewalk as she hurried to join the group.

"What's the status of the investigation, Deputy?" she asked in a crisp tone. "Why are you standing out here lollygagging when you ought to be looking for clues and tracking down suspects?"

"I'm working on it, Miz Lambert," Skip said. The words spilled out so quickly, he almost stuttered. "I'm conferring with Missus Hanlon right now."

"Good." Renee gave a decisive nod. "If kidnappings aren't solved within the first forty-eight hours, the likelihood of finding the victim diminishes rapidly. I've heard that time and again on *America's Most Wanted*, and we've already passed the forty-eight-hour mark. There's no time to waste."

"But that's with a kidnapping," Skip protested. "And this is a—"

"Tragic situation," Kate broke in, giving Skip a warning glare.

Skip swallowed and nodded. "Yes, ma'am. We're all doing the very best we can. Believe me, we're just as anxious to find your little dog as you are."

"We all want to see him home again," Paul said reassuringly.

"Hey, Skip!" Carl Wilson trotted toward them from the direction of the Town Green. "I've been looking for you. I went over to your office at the Town Hall, and they told me I might find you on patrol."

Skip's face took on a more official demeanor. "What's the problem?"

"I need to report some vandalism."

"What?" Skip's reddish eyebrows shot up. "How much damage was done?"

Carl shrugged. "No damage, really. It's just that I came home for lunch and found the whole front of the house decorated with ..."

His gaze shifted from Skip to Kate and Paul to Renee, then back to Skip. "You know, with long strips of tissue."

"You mean the place was TP'd?" Kate bit back a smile at Carl's surprised expression.

"Kate and I raised three youngsters," Paul chuckled, "and their friends papered our house on occasion. We're familiar with the term."

Carl grinned and looked relieved. "Yeah, that's exactly what happened. I left for work early this morning, before sunup. I had a customer coming in to pick up his car today, and I needed to finish the job before he showed up. The house was probably 'decorated' last night, but I just didn't notice it in the dark."

"That's outrageous." Renee curled her lip. "Why would anyone want to engage in such disgusting behavior?"

Carl rubbed the back of his neck. "Like I said, there's no damage. It was probably just kids. I guess I'm more irritated than anything. I'd been planning on taking Scout to a dog-show workshop right after work, but that isn't going to happen now."

Renee sniffed indignantly. "Just because your cocker spaniel won that dog-food contest doesn't mean you can expect her to do well in a conformation class."

"Yes, ma'am. I mean, no, ma'am." Carl eyed Renee warily, then went on. "I just came home to grab a quick bite and saw the mess as soon as I drove up to the house. I got most of the loose stuff picked up so it won't blow around the neighborhood, but I'm due back at work right away. My brother Jack would help with the cleanup if he was around, but he's out of town for a couple of days, so I'll have a lot to do after I get off work."

He smiled ruefully. "Hearing myself talk about it, it doesn't seem like that big a deal. Maybe I just needed to blow off some steam. I probably shouldn't have even bothered you with it."

"No," Skip said, "you did the right thing. It's important for me to know when something like this happens in our town. Come on, my SUV's parked right down the block. You can tell me more about it while we drive to your house. At least I can take a report and see if there's any indication of who might have done it."

"Thanks." Carl clapped him on the shoulder.

Renee's eyes glittered. "Don't forget where your priorities lie, deputy. A littered yard can hardly compare with Kisses being stolen."

"I won't forget, Miz Lambert. You can trust me on that." Skip sketched a wave to the others as the two men set off toward his patrol vehicle.

Kate stared after them, her mind in a whirl. *Dognapping? Vandalism? What was going on in Copper Mill?*

She looked over at the woman beside her. Renee seemed to have recovered from her breakdown the previous Saturday, but Kate noted the telltale signs of grief that still marked her features. And something else was different, but what?

Irritated by her inability to put her finger on it, Kate gave an impatient sniff . . . and then she knew. Her nose hadn't picked up the slightest whiff of Estée Lauder's Youth-Dew. Normally Renee would have been enveloped by a cloud of her signature perfume, but not this afternoon.

Kate eyed Renee more closely, wondering if her brisk demeanor was no more than a thin veneer. "How are you holding up?" Kate asked.

Renee twisted the ring on her right hand. "I'm staying busy. I just need to get my Little Umpkins back." She looked squarely at Kate. "What about you? Any progress?"

Kate shook her head slowly. "I'm sorry, Renee. I'm doing everything I can think of, but I just haven't come up with anything yet. I won't give up, though. I can promise you that."

"And you have prayer on your side," Paul added. "I'm not the sleuth Kate is, but I'll do everything I can in that department." He took Kate's elbow, and they started moving toward the car.

"Just a minute." Renee raised her hand like a police officer halting traffic. She opened the Oldsmobile's passenger door and reached inside, pulling out an armload of flyers.

"I told you I've been busy." She held up the flyers so that Kate and Paul could get a clear view of the top sheet.

An enlarged image of Kisses took up most of the upper half of the page. At the top of the flyer, the word *Kidnapped* stretched across the page in enormous block letters.

Directly beneath the photo was the question, "Have you seen this dog?" followed by Kisses' name and a detailed description, including his height, weight, and distinguishing characteristics—"sweet disposition, loves chopped liver."

Kate read the rest of the wording out loud: "My precious baby was abducted from Copper Mill Park. Please help me find him so I can bring him home. If you have any information as to his whereabouts or the identity of the perpetrators of this heinous crime, please call any of the following . . ."

Phone numbers were listed for Renee, the deputy's office in Copper Mill, and the sheriff's office in Pine Ridge. At the bottom of the page, large red letters proclaimed *Reward*.

"What do you think?" Renee asked. "I had them printed at the copy shop in Pine Ridge. I just picked them up an hour ago."

Kate's eyes stung, and her throat tightened. While some of the verbiage might have been a little over the top, it was easy to discern the depth of emotion that lay beneath it.

"I think they're very nice, don't you, Paul?"

"It definitely gets the message across," he agreed. "And you have quite a few of them."

"I have plans for every one." Renee shoved the stack into Kate's arms and reached back into the Oldsmobile. This time she brought out two large sketches.

She pointed to the one on top. "While I was waiting for the printer to finish up, I made a diagram of the streets in Copper Mill. These X's indicate the locations where I want the flyers posted."

Kate's eyes widened. "Very efficient. It looks like you're going to cover every storefront and lamppost in town."

"That's the idea." Renee pulled the second sketch from underneath the first. "I did the same thing for Pine Ridge, since it's just up the road. I intend to cover all the bases. That's why I'm glad I ran into you."

Renee thrust the diagrams at Paul, then dove back into the Oldsmobile for a third time, emerging with a roll of clear packing tape and a staple gun. "I've got to hurry straight back home. I need to stay by the phone in case there's a ransom call."

"Ransom?" Furrows appeared in Paul's forehead. "Renee, do you really think—"

She placed the tape and the staple gun on top of the stack of flyers Kate was holding. "If you get started right away and keep up a good pace, you should be able to have them all up by sundown."

Kate grimaced inwardly. Sunset in late summer came somewhere between eight thirty and nine.

"We ought to talk about this," she began.

Renee slammed the passenger door shut and circled around the front of the car. "I knew you'd be happy to do it, knowing that Kisses thinks of you as his grandma. Take good care of those diagrams. I plan to use them as a checklist to make sure all of the flyers are still in place. You can drop them off at my house when you're finished. Don't worry about disturbing me. I'm sure I'll be up late."

Kate stood with her mouth open as the pink

Oldsmobile backed out of the parking space and headed down Smith Street. She turned to Paul. "What just happened?"

Paul covered his mouth with his hand, but not quite in time to hide a broad smile. "It looks like we've just signed on for a very busy afternoon and evening, Grandma. We'd better get moving."

Kate glanced down at the flyers, where Kisses' wistful little face stared up at her. She looked back up at Paul and made a face. "*Dog days*, indeed."

Chapter Seven

The following afternoon found Kate fanning her face with the skirt of her apron and wondering about the wisdom of spending time in the kitchen on such a sultry day. But she needed to think, and somehow in the act of baking, she found it easier to work through any puzzle she was trying to solve.

Besides, those cookie recipes in the pull-out section of the magazine she'd purchased the previous Saturday were just begging to be tested. Several of them had caught her eye, but even in her present mood, she just couldn't bring herself to heat up the kitchen if it wasn't absolutely necessary.

Upon closer inspection of the magazine, she found a number of no-bake recipes. After scanning the most promising ones and checking them against the ingredients she had on hand, she decided on one that looked particularly interesting.

Kate pulled out butter, chocolate chips, walnuts, colored mini-marshmallows, and coconut, and soon the baking—or nonbaking—project was underway. As she heated the butter and chocolate chips in the top of her double boiler, she felt a twinge of guilt for following her culinary inclinations rather than being out searching for Kisses.

But where could she begin? She had talked to everyone who crossed her path while she hung up the flyers the previous afternoon, but no one seemed to know anything that might be of help.

Kate pushed a damp strand of her strawberry-blonde hair off her forehead with the back of her hand. Maybe her mental logjam was the result of the stultifying effect of the heat. Or maybe there just wasn't anything to be found—a sobering thought.

She removed the melted butter and chocolate chips from the heat and let them cool while she tossed the pastel-colored marshmallows and the nuts in a mixing bowl.

What could have happened to Kisses?

Kate poured the chocolate mixture over the marshmallows and stirred the sticky concoction. Even if someone was really angry with Renee, making her go through that kind of misery and causing an innocent animal distress—or worse—seemed excessive. Kate knew that jealousy, even rivalry, made people do some pretty outrageous things, but she couldn't imagine anyone taking things to such an extreme.

Then again, after reading the dog magazine and watching a couple of the shows Livvy had recommended on *Animal Planet*, Kate had learned more than she wanted to about the highly competitive nature of these events.

Kate sprinkled several sheets of waxed paper with grated coconut. She divided the dough and placed a lump on each sheet, then she rolled the dough into coconut-coated logs. While her hands were busy, her mind continued to work out the possible trails that might lead her to Kisses.

If not rivalry or jealousy, what other reason could there be to take Renee's Chihuahua? She'd already considered the three top motives: greed, hatred, and revenge. She hadn't ruled them out yet, but she was hoping for a less unpleasant scenario that would explain Kisses' disappearance.

She slid the dough logs onto a baking sheet and placed it in the refrigerator to chill, then she washed her hands. She had done some checking on the Internet and found that a pedigreed Chihuahua could command a substantial price.

Kisses did have papers, but those were in Renee's possession, not the dognapper's. According to Kate's research, the going price for a Chihuahua without papers would fall into a much lower category.

Kate poured herself a tall ice-cold glass of sun tea and drank deeply. If someone with a criminal bent wanted to make quick money, surely he could have found a more lucrative opportunity.

Then there was a possibility she'd already considered: If Kisses had been curled up inside his new bag, a random dognapper wouldn't have seen him, and it was unlikely that a purse snatcher would have made off with the tote once he saw Kisses inside.

That line of reasoning argued against some chance snatch and run and pointed back to someone deliberately trailing Renee, watching her movements closely with the intent to make off with Kisses. Kate mulled over this unpleasant likelihood while she stacked her utensils in the sink.

How were the cookies doing? She peeked in the fridge, knowing full well they hadn't had time to set properly but longing to know how the new recipe had turned out. She pulled out one of the logs and prodded it with her forefinger. Still far too soft to slice as the recipe instructed, but it wouldn't hurt to take a little taste test.

She peeled the waxed paper back from one end and held the roll firmly while she cut off a small chunk as neatly as she could. Kate smiled at the results. The colored chunks of marshmallow interlaced with veins of chocolate reminded her of one of her stained-glass windows. She popped the bite into her mouth and chewed the gooey morsel slowly. The varying flavors and textures of chocolate, marshmallow, coconut, and walnuts delighted her taste buds. Yes, this recipe would definitely be a keeper.

Think now, eat later. Kate brought her focus back to the missing-dog mystery.

She decided to reconsider jealousy as a possible motive. The other dog-club members certainly made ideal suspects, but she still couldn't bring herself to believe that one dog lover would inflict such agony on another.

Kate ran hot water into the mixing bowl and added a

squirt of dish detergent. Few things about the situation made sense. But the fact remained that Kisses was missing. He didn't wander off; he was intentionally taken while he was asleep in his tote.

Kate felt sorely tempted to call Skip and see if he had come up with any new leads, but he'd already fielded enough phone calls from Renee. Besides, she thought he might ask her if she'd thought of anything new, and she would have nothing to tell him.

Kate leaned her elbows on the kitchen counter and sighed, feeling the weight of responsibility bear down upon her. Renee and Skip were both counting on her, and she was letting them down.

She closed her eyes and whispered, "Lord, none of us knows where Kisses is, except the person who took him—and you. Please help us find him."

A sense of peace filled her. Jesus told his disciples that God knew when a sparrow fell to the ground. Surely that meant he had his eye on Kisses as well. And none of this had taken the Lord by surprise, Kate reflected as she washed up the bowl and utensils. He had known this would happen long before it actually occurred.

And he had the situation completely under control. Excitement stirred within her at the thought.

In fact, she could already see signs that he was at work, even down to the smallest details, like Renee asking her to help out with the dog show. If Kate hadn't attended the dog-club meeting, she never would have realized how passionate people could become about this sort of thing.

She smiled as she dried her cooking utensils and started putting them away. If God had guided her this far, she could trust him to keep leading her every step of the way.

Kate laughed at the thought of her earlier dilemma about whether she should help out with the dog show. At the time, the decision had seemed so monumental, but reality had a way of shrinking things down to their proper size. Kate froze in the act of closing the drawer where she kept her measuring cups. An image of herself walking along Copper Mill Creek filled her mind, almost as if she were actually standing there instead of in her own kitchen.

She squeezed her eyes shut again and shook her head. What had prompted this vivid picture?

"Is there something you're trying to tell me, Lord?"

Kate put the mixing bowl back in the cupboard while she retraced her Monday afternoon walk step-by-step.

What was it that had tickled her memory so? She remembered walking and praying, rounding the curve in the creek, and drawing nearer to the bridge . . .

The bridge! Kate gasped. Scenes sped through her mind like a video on fast-forward. The angry voices, Brenna Phillips, the object that fell into the creek with a loud splash.

Kate sucked in her breath. Did it have something to do with the object that had fallen into the water?

She closed her eyes and replayed the incident, remembering the flash of white as it plummeted toward the water. Kate's eyes flew open, and she pressed her hands against her mouth.

Kisses' new tote was white.

Alarm bells went off in her head. Surely she hadn't seen Kisses' tote plunging into the creek! Or worse, the tote with Kisses *in* it. Her breath caught. Could she have witnessed Brenna's companion—or partner in crime—getting rid of the evidence? Kate swallowed hard against the knot of fear that rose in her throat. Could it be that Kisses wasn't just missing but was gone altogether?

Tears welled in Kate's eyes as she envisioned the devastating effect it would have on Renee. And on her, if she was honest.

But such a scenario would mean that Brenna Phillips had been involved with Kisses' disappearance. Kate shook her head in disbelief. Being involved in a criminal act seemed completely out of character for the cheerful teen who seemed to be making such progress in her spiritual walk.

Kate checked the cookies and decided she could try slicing them again. This time the knife cut through the log more cleanly, and the slices bore an even more striking resemblance to tiny stained-glass windows. She set half the cookies on a serving tray and arranged the other half on a decorative plastic plate. She would take the plate to Renee and enjoy the rest with Paul later that evening.

The scene on the bridge haunted her thoughts. *Could sweet, lively Brenna Phillips really be a part of something as ugly as a dognapping?*

Every one of us is only a step away from doing something wrong. The words from one of Paul's sermons on grace echoed through her mind. It was possible that Brenna had made a bad choice that had led her into an activity she would normally have no part in. And if that was the case . . .

Should she tell Skip about her suspicions? The thought of implicating Brenna without proof made Kate's stomach turn.

If only she could know for sure whether Brenna had any connection to Kisses' disappearance. Kate weighed her options and came to a decision. She would go back to the bridge and look around, see if she could find something to put her concerns to rest.

She stretched a length of clear plastic wrap over each batch of cookies and carried the plastic plate with her on her way to get her keys and handbag.

She'd take the cookies to Renee, then backtrack to the creek to do some sleuthing. Even if she didn't have any progress to report to Renee, she could at least offer support and reassurance. And she could ask whether Renee had received any calls in response to her flyers.

AFTER DROPPING OFF the cookies at Renee's house, Kate felt an even stronger sense of urgency about locating Kisses quickly. The flyers hadn't brought in any response, and Renee's despondency was deeper than before.

Kate parked her Accord in the same place she'd parked two days before and retraced her steps along the creekside path. She wasn't entirely certain what she was looking for, but she felt sure she'd know it when she saw it.

She slowed as she reached the serviceberry bush that screened the bridge from sight and tried to recreate the scene in her mind. She'd become aware of the voices by the time she had reached that point.

Kate stopped and looked along the edge of the creek to where it rounded the bend past the bush, trying to get a sense of whether anything appeared different.

It all looked the same to her. Water trickled over the rocks, and sunlight dappled the ground. She could see nothing unusual, certainly nothing to spark any interest.

She stepped around the serviceberry bush and made her way toward the bridge.

Which side had that white object gone over? She couldn't be sure. She had only gotten a quick impression, a flash caught out of the corner of her eye. Not enough to imprint any details in her mind.

Kate halted about fifteen feet from the bridge and studied it carefully. She couldn't see any telltale white threads snagged on the railing.

Maybe she would have more success on the bridge itself. Kate approached the bridge and walked onto it for a closer look.

Brenna stood about . . . here. Kate had never been able to get a clear view of the second person on the bridge. Who had thrown the object—whatever it was—into the creek?

She examined the length of the railing on both sides, then the boards under her feet. Once again, her search yielded nothing.

Before she descended to ground level, she stood in the center of the bridge looking downstream. Nothing unusual stood out, so she returned to the creek bank and continued.

Kate searched the bank, the rocks, any clumps of grass where something flung over the side of the bridge might have caught and held.

In a couple of places, she spotted clumps of debris and a few empty soda cans that lay in the clefts along the bank, caught by the swirling water. But no white leather tote, and no little dog.

Kate didn't know whether to be relieved or disappointed. She still wasn't any closer to determining what she had seen that day, but at least there wasn't any evidence that Kisses had met his doom on that spot, and for that she was grateful.

Of course, she couldn't be positive the tote hadn't been tossed over the bridge. Kate wondered how far a leather tote would float downstream. And would it have been watertight? Would Kisses have been protected while sailing down the creek like baby Moses in his papyrus basket? That is, if Kisses had still been in the tote. Whoever stole Kisses may have taken him out of the tote before getting rid of the evidence. She stood on the edge of the bank and stared downstream.

"Kisses, where are you?"

More thoughts filtered through her mind. If the person who took Kisses still had him, was the little dog being well cared for?

Kisses was used to a pampered existence and constant affection and protection. Was he being neglected or abused? Was he locked up in a cage? What was happening to him right then?

With an effort, Kate put the brakes on her gloomy musing. Renee's overactive imagination must have been rubbing off on her.

She turned back and followed the path to her car, feeling somewhat dejected. She hadn't found Kisses; neither had she found anything that pointed to Brenna's guilt. Then again, she hadn't discovered anything to exonerate the teen either.

Still, she hesitated calling Skip Spencer to point an accusing finger at a sweet young girl who might not have done anything wrong.

This wasn't a decision she wanted to make on her own. She needed to talk to Paul.

Just thinking about sharing the burden with him made it seem lighter. Paul would give her wise advice. Kate decided she'd talk to him after choir practice.

"HAVE YOU EVER RUN ACROSS a family named Newcomb?" Paul asked when Kate returned home from practice that night.

Kate shook her head and crossed the living room. She moved a throw pillow out of her way and sank onto the couch.

"No, that name isn't familiar. Why?" She patted the cushion next to her.

Paul joined her and slipped his arm around her shoulders. "A fellow named Daniel Newcomb came into the church a couple of days ago looking for work, and I'd really like to find out more about his situation. Maybe we can find a way to help him."

He told Kate about the trouble Daniel had keeping a job.

"He's a nice young man, but he seems desperate to make some money. He's got a wife, two kids, and a puppy to support.

"He's under a lot of stress. I think he just needs a listening ear. I'd like to get to know him better."

Kate snuggled closer. "If a listening ear is what he needs, he went to the right place." She grinned. "In fact, I need a listening ear right now. I'm really torn about something I saw, and I need to hear your thoughts on it."

Paul tightened his arm around her shoulder. "Sure, hon. What's up?"

"Remember when Skip asked me if I had any idea who could have taken Kisses?"

Paul nodded. "You told him you didn't."

"I still don't. Not really, anyway." Kate turned so she could look up at Paul. "But I'm wondering if I might have stumbled across a lead."

She recounted what she'd seen and heard at the bridge the previous Monday. "I went back today, looking for something that would give me some clue as to whether

Brenna might be involved in this. I hoped that if it was Renee's tote I saw falling from the bridge, there might be a scrap of leather or some thread caught on the bridge or floating in the water—some clue to let me know one way or the other."

Interest flickered in Paul's eyes. "And what did you find?"

"Nothing. Not a scrap of leather, not a sign of Kisses, not a single thing. I don't have evidence of any wrongdoing. I don't know for sure if what I saw has any connection with Kisses' disappearance. But the timing makes me wonder."

"I see your dilemma. You don't want to withhold evidence that could help Skip in his investigation, but you don't want to accuse Brenna unjustly."

"That's just it," Kate said miserably. She slipped out of Paul's arms and turned so she was facing him. "I don't know whether I have information worth passing along or not. Do I have any right to implicate Brenna without proof?"

Paul drew in a deep breath and let it out in a long sigh. "That's a tough one. Let me ask you this: What would you do if you did have evidence that pointed to Brenna's involvement?"

Kate didn't hesitate. "Like it or not, I'd have to tell Skip."

Paul nodded. "The way I see it, you have a clue that might lead to solving a crime. Determining whether it's important isn't up to you. Working that out is up to Skip.

Let law enforcement do its job. With no other leads, you've got to be willing to take the chance of being wrong if it turns out there is a connection."

"I know. I just don't want to cause trouble for Brenna. On the other hand, if she was involved in Kisses' disappearance, I'd want Skip to investigate. It might be the only way to find Kisses. But what if I'm wrong, and Brenna had nothing to do with it? I'm honestly not sure what to do."

Paul's clear blue eyes lit up when he smiled at her. "But I know someone who does. We need to pray about this."

"You are so right."

They joined hands and bowed their heads, and Kate lifted up a prayer for wisdom. Paul added a request of his own for God to work in whatever way he chose to bring Kisses back home.

When they lifted their heads, Kate squeezed his fingers tight. "That was exactly what I needed."

Paul reached out to stroke her cheek. "Feel better?"

Kate nodded. "I know what I'm supposed to do now. I need to tell Skip."

Chapter Eight

After Paul left for work the next morning, Kate picked up the phone and dialed the number for the deputy's office.

The dispatcher who answered told her that Skip was out on a call. "It shouldn't take long, though. Would you like me to take a message?"

"No, thanks," Kate said. "I'll call back later."

She spent the next hour in her studio working on a couple of small projects before making a second call to the deputy's office. This time Skip was in, so she drove into town, preferring to discuss such a sensitive matter face-to-face rather than over the phone.

Skip ushered Kate to a wooden chair near his desk and listened attentively while she told him what she'd seen and heard on Monday and about her unsuccessful attempt to find any corroborating evidence the previous day.

When she finished, he shook his head. "Well, it isn't much to go on. But since it's the only lead we have, I'd better check it out."

He stared off into space and drummed his fingers on the desktop for a moment, then looked back at Kate. "I'd hate to think that any of the kids around here would be involved in something like this. Then again, it might be just the kind of thing a kid could get himself—or herself—mixed up in, and then not know how to get out of."

Kate had to suppress a grin. Skip wasn't too many years older than the kids to whom he was referring, and yet here he was talking as if he were a gray-haired old man.

"I need to talk to Brenna," Skip continued. "Do you know offhand where she lives?"

"She and her mother live south of the Mercantile on Smith Street."

When Skip started to scoot his chair back, Kate held up her hand. "Brenna probably won't be home right now. She has a summer job at Emma's Ice Cream Shop, and Thursday is one of her days to work."

Skip hitched his chair forward and drummed his fingers on the desk again. "I'd hate to talk to her at work. Whether she has anything to do with this or not, my being there and questioning her would start a lot of talk. Brenna's never been in any trouble, but that doesn't matter much where gossip's concerned. Do you know what time she gets off work?"

"Usually around four thirty, or a bit after," Kate told him.

"I've called her a few times about youth-group activities, and if I remember right, she's usually home by five o'clock."

Skip nodded. "What about her mom?"

"Lisa works the day shift at Fancy Fabrics in Pine Ridge. She won't be home until five thirty or so."

Skip thought a moment. "That might work. It's not like I'm trying to get any incriminating information from her, and I don't want to stir up any trouble between Brenna and her mom."

He looked at Kate hesitantly. "Would you mind going with me? She'd probably feel more comfortable talking to me if you were around. Besides, I'd like her to hear the story straight from you."

Kate scribbled the address down on a scrap of paper and pushed it across the desk to Skip. "I can do that. Shall I meet you there around five?"

"That sounds good. I'll see you then."

Kate checked her watch and decided to swing by the library before heading home. She knew that Livvy had a budget meeting around lunchtime and probably wouldn't be up for an extended visit, but Kate felt the need to touch base with her friend, if only for a moment or two.

She found Livvy inside her office, going over some paperwork. Kate tapped on the door frame and waited until she looked up.

"I know you're busy, so I won't stay long. I just wanted to pop in and say hi."

Livvy dropped her pencil onto her desk and leaned back in her chair, stretching her arms wide. "Don't rush

off. I'm glad for the break. Having to deal with the budget
is one of my least favorite parts of the job, but I think I'll
have everything in order before the meeting.

"Anything new on Kisses?" Livvy gave Kate a wicked
grin. "I saw all the flyers papering the town. Let me guess.
You were recruited for manual labor on top of your detective duties?"

"A grandmother's work is never done," Kate quipped.
Both women laughed.

Kate settled into the chair opposite Livvy. "No one has
responded to the flyers yet. It's like the poor little dog
dropped off the face of the earth. To tell you the truth, I'm
stumped. I haven't turned up any solid leads. And Skip's
not having any more success than I am. There is . . ."

She started to mention Brenna's possible involvement,
then clamped her lips shut. That would be moving into
the realm of gossip, even with her closest friend.

"There's what?" Livvy asked.

Kate smiled and shook her head. "Oh, nothing. I was
just thinking out loud."

Livvy leaned forward and spoke in a quiet tone.
"*Hmm*. How long do you wait before giving up the search
for a missing dog? And the bigger question: what will it do
to Renee if he doesn't turn up?"

There it was, the question Kate had been trying to
avoid for days. Renee was in bad enough shape with
Kisses only listed as missing. Kate couldn't bear thinking
about what would happen if Renee found out he was gone
forever.

"I don't know," she admitted. "I haven't wanted to think that far ahead."

"I know what you mean," Livvy said. "She absolutely lives for that bug-eyed little dog. Is there anything I can do to help?"

"Keep your ears and eyes open. If anybody local was involved, someone around here has to know about it. See if anyone lets something slip." Kate rose to leave. "In the meantime, just keep praying."

Livvy got up and stepped around the desk to give Kate a warm squeeze. "You know I will."

Kate glanced at her watch as she walked down the library steps to her car. Just enough time to make a quick stop at the Mercantile for some lettuce before heading home to put together a chef's salad for lunch. Something filling but cool, perfect for a sultry summer day.

OVER LUNCH, Kate told Paul about her talk with Skip and his request that she be there when he interviewed Brenna later that day.

"That's probably a good idea," Paul agreed. "Having you there will make it seem less official."

Together they tried to brainstorm further ideas for finding some trace of Kisses, but Kate felt they were striking out at every turn.

"What about the man who stopped by the church the other day?" Kate asked, more than ready to switch to a subject that didn't involve a missing canine. "Did he come back again?"

"Daniel? No, I haven't seen him. Maybe he finally landed a new job. I hope that's the case. He has a lot of potential, though he doesn't seem to realize it. I believe he'll be able to make a success of things if he'll just give himself a chance."

He got up, then bent over to give Kate a kiss. "I'd better head back to the office now. I'll see you this evening after work. I left my day planner here in the study, and I've been at a loss without it all morning. I'd better grab it before I leave."

Paul headed for his study, and Kate began cleaning up from lunch. She had just filled the sink with hot, soapy water when the doorbell rang. Kate answered the door and found Renee standing on the porch holding a stack of pastel-colored sheets of paper.

Kate blinked at Renee's appearance. Her bleached-blonde hair, usually impeccably groomed, looked as if she'd barely bothered to comb it that morning. Her makeup had been hastily applied, and she wore a bright pink top with olive slacks, a combination Renee would never have chosen in a million years under normal circumstances.

But things were far from normal for Renee at the moment, Kate reminded herself. She suppressed a groan as she glanced at the pile of papers in Renee's hands. "More flyers?"

Without waiting for an invitation, Renee breezed past her into the living room just as Paul emerged from his study. "Oh, Paul, I'm glad you're home. I want you to see these too."

Paul flashed a questioning look at Kate, who shrugged her shoulders. Together they followed Renee to the coffee table. Kate noticed that this stack was far smaller than the one she'd been handed two days before.

"I don't intend for you to replace all of the flyers you put up the other day," Renee said, as if reading Kate's thoughts. "But I do want you to swap out some of the old flyers in the most strategic locations with these new ones. Now that we've passed that critical forty-eight-hour period, I feel we need to step things up a notch.

"It was important to get the other flyers up right away. But they show Kisses from only one angle. I want to put these up as well so the public will see Kisses in his different moods."

The flyers in this new batch were larger than the others, Kate noted, and were printed on heavier paper. The sheet on the top of the stack showed Kisses posed against a royal blue background, wearing a jeweled collar. Soft lighting feathered the focus, reminding Kate of a glamour shot.

"It's a beautiful photo," she began.

"I had all of them professionally done," Renee said with a catch in her voice. "I intend to put together a calendar with a different picture of Kisses each month as a special Christmas gift. I plan to call it A Year of Kisses."

Kate heard a muffled chuckle from Paul's direction and hoped Renee hadn't noticed. "What a lovely idea. I'm sure it will be much appreciated."

"You and Paul are getting one," Renee told her. "Two actually, one for your house and one for Paul's office at the church. It was supposed to be a surprise, but I thought it was more important to get these out to help further the search."

"What else do you have?" Kate asked, her curiosity getting the better of her.

Renee pulled the top flyer aside and gestured toward the one beneath. "This is Kisses in February."

Kate wouldn't have had any trouble figuring that out for herself, since the little dog sported a pink sweater with red hearts. An open box of chocolates sat beside him. Renee had even taken the time to glue ruffled lace around the edges of the flyer.

Renee looked at the picture and sighed. "My little valentine." She slid that one aside to reveal a shot of Kisses dressed in kelly green this time, perched atop a large rock.

Kate drew her eyebrows together. "I'm not sure—"

"Let me guess," Paul cut in. "It's Kisses on the Blarney stone, right?"

Kate elbowed him, but Renee's face lit up. "You figured it out! I wondered if my little joke would be too subtle. Yes, this is the photo for March."

Kate looked at Paul, then immediately glanced away, knowing that if their gazes met, they would both burst out laughing.

She tried to keep the mirth out of her voice. "Do you have all twelve months of the year here?"

"Yes." Renee proceeded to shuffle through the stack, pointing out one pose after another.

There was some holiday or seasonal connection with each one: Kisses dressed as Uncle Sam for July and in a Pilgrim hat for November. Renee had even put him in a little red suit and attached a tiny white beard to his chin for December. "I call that one Kisses Claus," she said with a tender smile.

She pulled the diagram of Copper Mill from under the last photo and spread it open on the table.

"I've amended the map to indicate where these new posters will go. Since there are only twelve of them, I wanted to pick the most effective spots around town." She pointed to various spots on the diagram where the new locations were marked with red X's.

"Well, they'll surely draw attention," Paul said.

"Good, I'm glad you approve." Renee turned to Kate. "You still have the tape and the staple gun, right?"

"Yes, let me go get them. I should have returned them before now." Kate took one step toward the study, but Renee laid a restraining hand on her arm.

"Oh no, not yet. You'll need them when you put these up this afternoon."

"But Renee, I—"

It was too late. Renee had already released Kate's arm and was on her way to the front door. She stopped long enough to call back, "I'm off now to get an update on the investigation from Deputy Spencer ... if he's in his office. If not, I'll track him down. I do believe that young man has been avoiding me."

Renee toodled her fingers at them before heading out

the door. After the door had closed behind her, Kate sagged against Paul's chest, and they both dissolved into helpless laughter.

Paul recovered first. "It really isn't funny, but those photos! Only Renee would come up with something like that."

"I know." Kate wiped tears from her eyes. "You have to give her credit for doing her best, though. And I guess I know how I'll be spending my afternoon before I meet Skip at Brenna's house."

Chapter Nine

Having put up the last of Renee's new flyers— Kisses wearing Hawaiian swim trunks for June —Kate pulled her Honda alongside the curb in front of the Phillips' house at two minutes to five. When Skip pulled up behind her a moment later, she got out of the car and walked over to him.

"Is she home yet?" he asked.

"I assume so, but I didn't check," Kate told him. "I was waiting for you." She felt a flutter of nervousness as they followed the cracked concrete walk up to the rundown blue house.

From a closer perspective, Kate could see peeling paint on the white shutters and mesh that had pulled away from one corner of the screen door—signs that Lisa didn't have the time or resources for these minor repairs.

With a car that was continually falling apart and a house that didn't look too far behind, Lisa certainly had more than her share of stressors on her plate. Kate wondered if she and Skip were about to add another.

Skip gave a series of sharp raps on the screen door and stepped back behind Kate. Kate could hear the sound of footsteps crossing the hardwood floor.

Brenna pulled the front door open a crack and peered outside. She grinned when she saw Kate. "Hi, Mrs. Hanlon. What's up?"

Her gaze shifted past Kate to Skip, and the grin slid from her face. Her eyes grew round, and her hand clutched the door frame. She looked back at Kate, the color draining from her face. "What's going on? Did something happen to my mom?"

"Oh, honey, no," Kate was quick to assure her. If not for the screen door between them, Kate would have reached out and folded the frightened girl in her arms.

She gave Brenna an encouraging smile. "It's nothing like that. We just wanted to talk with you for a minute, if that's all right."

"Okay." Brenna's gaze swung from Kate to Skip, then back again as if she wasn't completely sure about Kate's answer. "You'd better come in then." She pushed open the screen door, which creaked loudly, and ushered them into a small living room.

"Have a seat." Brenna gestured toward the couch, then hurried to snatch up a red-and-white-striped apron that lay draped across the arm of a chair. Kate could see "Emma's Ice Cream" embroidered on the bib in bright blue letters.

"Sorry," Brenna said. "I just got home from work a few minutes ago. I'll be back in a second."

She trotted down a short hallway and tossed the apron through an open doorway into what Kate assumed was her bedroom, then the teen came back and perched on a chair opposite the couch.

Kate sat on the edge of the couch and smiled. "Are you enjoying your job?"

"Yeah. I wanted to prove to my mom that I'm more responsible than she thinks I am, and it seems to be working." She paused and shifted nervously in her chair. "So what did you want to talk to me about?"

Skip leaned forward with his arms on his knees. Kate appreciated his efforts not to frighten Brenna by looking overly official. "We just need to ask you a couple of questions about something Mrs. Hanlon saw the other day."

Brenna tilted her head and looked at Kate, obviously puzzled.

Kate pressed the palms of her hands together in her lap and took a deep breath. The sooner she got this over with, the sooner everything could be cleared up.

"Well, I was taking a walk along the creek on Monday afternoon."

Brenna nodded, still looking mystified.

"I was up near the bridge when I heard voices. It sounded like people arguing."

Something flickered in Brenna's eyes. She drew her feet back under her chair and laced her fingers together in her lap.

Kate went on, watching the girl closely. "I didn't get close enough to hear what was said, and I didn't want to intrude, so I turned away to go back to my car. But as I did, I saw something that made me curious."

Brenna pulled back farther into her chair, looking as though she wished she were anywhere but there. Her lips tightened, and she swallowed hard.

Kate sighed. This wasn't getting any easier. She looked the dark-haired girl straight in the eyes. "While I didn't hear what was being said, I was able to see one of the people on the bridge. I recognized you, Brenna."

"You were spying on me, Mrs. Hanlon?"

"Of course not." Kate's eyes widened in surprise. "I had no idea you were there until I overheard the voices and saw you through some branches."

Brenna drew a long, shaky breath. "Yeah, that was me on the bridge, but I don't see—"

"Mrs. Hanlon saw something fall off the bridge into the creek," Skip said. "What we need to know is, who was with you and what was tossed into the water?"

"But why is that anybody else's business?"

Skip's voice held a note of authority that impressed Kate. "You see, we're investigating the disappearance of Renee Lambert's dog, and we're trying to determine whether you know anything about it."

Brenna shook her head, as if trying to clear it. "You think I had something to do with that?"

The wounded look in her eyes stung Kate's heart, but she steeled herself. A crime had been committed, and it was important to get to the bottom of it.

"We're not saying you did," Kate said. "It's just that

whatever was dropped into the water was white, and the tote Mrs. Lambert carried Kisses in was white, and—"

Brenna sprang to her feet. "You think I'd drop a dog into the creek? No way, Mrs. Hanlon! You should know me better than that."

Kate heard footsteps hurrying up the walk. The next instant, the screen door screeched open, and Lisa Phillips rushed into the room.

"Brenna, what's wrong? Are you all right? I saw the deputy's SUV outside."

She skidded to a halt and stared at the scene before her. She looked at Brenna, who was red-faced and clearly upset, then she glared at Kate and Skip.

Lisa rushed over to her Brenna and put her arm around her daughter's shoulders. "What's going on here?"

Skip stood. "We just wanted to ask your daughter a few questions."

"Without me here? What about her legal rights?"

"There weren't any accusations made, ma'am. We were just trying to find out if she had any information about an incident we're looking into."

Lisa looked from Skip to Kate. "If this isn't some kind of emergency, I don't understand what the preacher's wife is doing here."

Kate got to her feet, praying that her knees would hold her up. "Like Skip said, we aren't accusing Brenna of any-thing. We were just asking about a conversation she had with someone on the bridge at Copper Mill Creek this past Monday."

"That and what they threw off the bridge," Skip added.

Lisa tightened her arm around her daughter's shoulders. "Okay, Brenna, who were you talking to?"

"It doesn't matter. It has nothing to do with Mrs. Lambert's dog being stolen."

Lisa's eyes widened. "You're saying that you think my daughter was involved in some kind of—"

"No, no. Nothing like that." Kate's heart sank. "We only wanted to know—"

"Let's get this straightened out once and for all," Lisa broke in. "Brenna, did you have anything to do with Mrs. Lambert's dog being stolen?"

Brenna shook her head. "No, Mom. You know I wouldn't do anything like that."

Lisa's eyes misted, and she gave Brenna a hug. "I know, honey, but apparently they don't. So who were you talking to, and what's all this about you throwing something off the bridge?"

Brenna shook her head, making her dark curls dance. "It doesn't have anything to do with this. Trust me, okay?"

Lisa gave her daughter a long look, then turned back to Kate and Skip. "You heard my daughter. She can't help you. I think it's time for you to leave."

Skip gave a polite nod and started toward the door.

Kate held back a moment, then she stepped toward the agitated woman. "Lisa, please believe me. I would never—"

Lisa cut her off with an upraised hand. "You've already said enough."

Kate followed Skip, feeling heartsick.

Lisa's voice carried through the screen door. "Now do you believe me, baby? Didn't I tell you, you can't trust church people?"

Skip waited, leaning against Kate's black Honda with his arms folded across his chest. "Well, that didn't do us much good."

"No," Kate agreed. "I think we stirred up more problems than we solved."

"You've got that right," Skip said mournfully. "I should have thought harder about coming out to talk to Brenna without her mother around. Sheriff Roberts is going to have my hide when he hears about that. It seems like the harder I try to prove to him that I'm a good investigator, the more trouble I get into."

He raked his fingers through his red hair. "For being such a little thing, that Chihuahua sure has created a big mess. If I don't find some way to get Miz Lambert off my back, I'll go crazy."

Kate managed a weak smile. "I'm sorry she's still putting pressure on you."

"And not just her, either. She sicced my mom on me the other day."

The radio on Skip's duty belt squawked, and he keyed the mic. "Spencer here."

The dispatcher's voice crackled over the airwaves. "Deputy, you'd better get over to the Philpotts' place. Lester just phoned in a report about a prowler."

Skip keyed the mic again. "I'm responding." He shook his head. "I'll talk to you later, Missus Hanlon. I've got to go."

"HERE WE'VE BEEN PRAYING that Lisa would draw closer to the Lord, and all I've managed to do is drive her farther away."

Kate reached for Paul's hand, and his fingers tightened around hers as they sauntered along Smoky Mountain Road. The evening was far too warm to do anything in a hurry.

"You did what you had to do," he reminded her. "And surely it was better for Brenna to have you along rather than for Skip to show up at her door alone."

"Maybe," Kate conceded. "But it certainly can't help her to see that kind of altercation between her mother and the pastor's wife." She told him what she overheard Lisa saying to Brenna.

Sadness shone in Paul's eyes. "I wonder what happened to destroy her trust in Christians."

"I don't know," Kate said, "but the bitterness I saw in her eyes tells me she's been deeply wounded somehow."

They walked along the fence line of a grassy pasture. A pair of horses whinnied and came over to them. One pushed his head over the top strand of fence wire and looked at Kate hopefully.

She stopped long enough to rub the bay's velvety nose, and the horse nuzzled against her hand.

"Sorry," she told him. "I don't have anything for you

today. Maybe next time I'll remember to tuck a carrot in my pocket."

The other horse was more standoffish, hanging back and watching with a wary expression.

Like Lisa's. The thought brought Kate back to the topic at hand.

She linked her fingers in Paul's again, and they walked on in silence for a few minutes before she said, "So, how do I fix what I did? Any ideas?"

"Not yet." He sighed. "We'll just have to try to befriend her and show her God's love."

Kate gave a short laugh. "I have a feeling that Lisa didn't take my actions today as very friendly."

"Maybe it's not for us to break down that barrier. Maybe we just need to ask God to raise up the right person to connect with Lisa and form a friendship that can get her past whatever's eating away at her."

Kate looked at Paul. "That doesn't mean we stop trying, though."

"Of course not. But we need to make sure we let God do it in his own way and his own time."

When they reached the far end of the pasture, they turned and began retracing their steps. Kate was glad she had prepared the filling for the chicken-pecan croissant sandwiches before they set off on their walk. After they got home, supper would take only a few minutes to put together so Paul could eat before he left for the men's prayer meeting.

"I know you'll have to eat and run," Kate said. "Could we pray about this as soon as you get home tonight?"

Paul smiled and wrapped his arm around her shoulder. "There's nothing to stop us from praying while we walk. Why don't we do it right now?"

So they did. As they prayed, Kate's heart swelled with gratitude. No matter what the problem, she could always count on Paul's love and support— and godly example.

I am so blessed, she told herself as she squeezed Paul's hand.

Chapter Ten

Paul surveyed the bookshelf in his church office. He'd just had that book of quotations out the other day; where had he put it? He ran his finger along the titles on the top shelf, then the second, past commentaries and volumes on counseling.

Ah, there it was! He smiled and slid the thick book from its place. He had found the perfect quotation to use in the following day's sermon, but he'd neglected to write it down.

He hefted the volume in his hand, flipped it open to the required quote, then began copying it onto a notepad.

"Pastor, are you in here?"

Paul drew up, startled by the unexpected voice. He ducked his head for a quick look out the window and saw Daniel Newcomb's gray Blazer parked next to his Chevy pickup.

Paul stepped into the outer office and held his hand out to the younger man. "Daniel, good to see you! How have you been? Have you found that new job yet?"

Daniel shoved his hands into his front pockets. "No, not yet. I've been lookin', though. Actually, that's why I stopped by. You said you might want me to come back and take a whack at that kudzu."

"Sure, that would be great." Paul took in the man's appearance with a quick glance. Daniel's jeans didn't look any less tattered than they had during his previous visit. In fact, Paul wasn't sure they weren't the same pair. His T-shirt was a faded red this time, and light-blond stubble showed on his cheeks and chin. Paul wondered whether he'd eaten a square meal since their earlier conversation.

"I'm glad you caught me," he said, walking back to his desk to retrieve the key to the shed. "We'll find the tools you need and get you started." He headed toward the outer door, expecting Daniel to follow, but the younger man didn't move.

"Can I ask you something?"

"Sure." Paul turned back and leaned against Millie's desk, careful not to disturb the stack of papers in one corner. The finicky secretary would have his hide if she saw anything out of order when she came to work on Monday. Sometimes he wondered if she realized who was the employer and who was the employee.

He looked at Daniel. "What would you like to know?"

"The other day you said you thought I seemed like a hard worker."

Daniel dropped his gaze and shifted from one foot to the other, then looked back up at Paul. "Did you mean that? Do you really think I can get my act together and turn my life around?"

"Yes, I meant it. You strike me as a young man with plenty of potential, but you have to make the right choices and stick by them."

Daniel's forehead crinkled. "What kind of choices are you talking about?"

Paul pursed his lips, then waved toward his office. "Why don't we talk in here?"

He motioned for the young man to take a seat in one of the visitor's chairs, then he pulled another chair over so he and Daniel could sit face-to-face without the desk creating a barrier between them.

Daniel parked himself on the edge of the chair. "You looked like you were gettin' ready to leave. I don't want to take up your whole Saturday morning."

"That's not a problem. My wife is at a meeting. I'm going to finish up my sermon for tomorrow, but that's all I have planned until she gets home."

Paul rested his elbows on the arms of his chair and steepled his fingers. "So, let's talk about choices. Every morning when you wake up, you have to recognize that you have the choice to go to work, do the job to the best of your ability, and make your employer happy with the way you do it."

"But that's what I try to do," Daniel protested. "Every time I go in thinkin' I'm gonna do the best job I can, but somehow it never works out that way."

"Why do your employers get upset with you?"

Daniel scrunched up his face in thought. "I don't know. I try my best, but my best isn't good enough. I do what I think they told me to do, and then they tell me I did it wrong. It's like nobody takes the time to show me how to do it the way they want."

He shrugged his shoulders. "I don't know. Maybe I'm not smart enough for these jobs. Most of the time, I just feel stupid. Maybe my wife's parents were right all along."

Paul saw a faint sheen of moisture in the other man's eyes and knew the conversation had just struck a nerve. He probed a little further, treading carefully. "You don't get along with your in-laws?"

Daniel blew out a puff of air. "I don't see them often enough to get along or not, and that's just fine with me. They told my wife she was makin' a big mistake marrying me, and I'd never amount to anything."

He slumped in the chair and hung his head. "Maybe they were right."

Paul leaned forward, his elbows on his knees. "Daniel, how do you think God sees you? Do you really think he brought you into this world just to be a failure?"

Daniel shook his head, then nodded, then shrugged. He looked up, and Paul winced at the anguish he saw in the young man's eyes.

"That's all they think I am. They told Crystal she married down."

Paul stared at him. "Down?"

"Beneath herself," Daniel explained. "Said I wasn't good enough for her, and someday she'd regret pickin' a loser like me. That's one reason why I haven't told her yet that I've lost another job."

Paul sat bolt upright. "She doesn't know?"

Daniel shook his head, looking utterly miserable. "She knows I've been out of sorts lately. Moody, she calls it. But she doesn't know why. Not yet, anyway. I guess I can't put off tellin' her forever."

"No, you can't." Paul ran his fingers through his hair. "How long do you think you can keep something like this from her? I can't imagine how you've managed it this long."

A haunted expression flittered across Daniel's face. "I've been keepin' to my usual schedule. She thinks I've been going to work like always, but I've been knockin' on doors and fillin' out applications instead. Sometimes doing little odd jobs to bring in a few dollars, like I did for you the other day. As long as I leave and get home at the regular times, she hasn't clued in to what's really going on."

"Aren't you afraid she'll come into town sometime and see you out pounding the pavement when she thinks you're at work?"

Daniel gave him a shamefaced grin. "That's one thing I don't have to worry about. We've only got the one SUV, so Crystal doesn't come into town on her own. She wouldn't have many people to visit here even if she did. She spends all her time takin' care of the kids. They keep her hoppin' from morning till night."

His face softened. "She really is something special. I don't know why she ever took up with a guy like me."

"I doubt she sees it that way. How long have you been married?"

"Eight years. It took us a while before we had kids. She worked as a checker at Kroger in Memphis until our little boy was born almost four years ago. Then our baby girl came along a couple of years after that, and Crystal's stayed home takin' care of them ever since."

He grinned proudly. "She says she likes bein' a stay-at-home mom. She'd like to have a whole mess of kids. Sometimes she teases me about havin' half a dozen or so."

His grin faded, and he snorted. "I can barely put food on the table for the two we have now. Pretty soon, what little cash I've got is going to be used up and gone if things don't change."

Moisture filmed his eyes again. "Crystal's stuck with me all these years and never said a word about me goin' from job to job. But I'm afraid this may turn out to be the last straw that'll open her eyes and let her see that her parents were right."

His Adam's apple bobbed up and down. "I don't want to think what would happen if I went home someday and found out she'd packed up and taken the kids back to her mom and dad. It'd just kill me."

Paul spoke gently but with conviction. "Daniel, God loves you. He doesn't want you to feel this way about yourself, and he doesn't want your family to be broken apart either. What we've got to do is find out what God does have for you. And you can't keep on deceiving your wife. You're going to have to let her know what's going on. Why don't we pray now and ask God to show you the job he created you for?"

Daniel sniffed and swiped at his eyes. "You think there really is a job like that?"

"Only God knows. The best thing you can do is to trust him, because he's the one who made you, and he knows what's inside you. What I see when I look at you is an honest, hard-working man who needs to discover what his true purpose is."

Daniel straightened his shoulders, and a light of hope shone in his eyes. "Pastor, if praying works, I'm game."

"WHY, MRS. HANLON. What a surprise." Wilbur Dodson blinked when Kate entered the meeting room on the library's second floor.

Kate let the glass door close behind her and slid into the nearest seat. Velma and Lucy Mae each gave her a curious glance, then looked away.

Wilbur cleared his throat, making a sound like dry leaves rustling in an autumn wind. "I applaud your willingness to be here, even though our meetings are more geared toward club officials rather than . . . ancillary staff."

Kate chose not to take the bait. She smiled politely at Wilbur and wiggled her fingers at Lucy Mae.

Wilbur cleared his throat again. Lucy Mae snapped to attention and looked back down at the sheet in front of her.

"Arlo Sanders?"

"Here," called a beefy, red-faced man.

Lucy Mae marked the sheet.

"Renee Lambert?"

Wilbur turned to Lucy Mae. "I think we must take it as a given that Renee is too preoccupied to join us today."

Lucy Mae nodded. "Then I'll just mark it down as"—she ran her finger down the sheet—"seven members present."

"And one guest." Wilbur looked at Kate and sighed.

Kate maintained her smile, ignoring the implied reproof in Wilbur's tone.

The club president stared at her a moment longer, then rapped his knuckles on the table and continued the meeting.

Kate settled back in her chair and watched the proceedings. She had a twofold purpose in attending the meeting that week. One was to learn more about the organization and preparations for the dog show and her part in it.

The other more pressing reason was to take advantage of this opportunity to observe the club members and see if any of them stood out as a likely suspect in Kisses' disappearance.

Without Bud Barkley to hijack the agenda, Wilbur was able to keep the meeting running along at a steady clip. He seemed much more relaxed and sure of himself than he'd been the week before.

Various members gave reports on motel reservations for the show judges, the delivery of portable restrooms to the show site, and the name of the vet who would be on standby for the duration of the show.

While they talked, Kate watched each one and listened carefully, on the alert for any flicker of expression or slip of the tongue that might be an indicator of guilt. But try as she might, she couldn't discern anything out of the ordinary.

Following the reports came a prolonged discussion of the most advantageous placement of the bleachers at the event. Then the agenda shifted to the show awards, and Velma volunteered to pick them up from the engraver in Pine Ridge when they were ready.

Wilbur looked at his watch and announced, "Well, I think that about—"

Lucy Mae cleared her throat and said in a low voice, "Check your agenda."

Wilbur looked down at the sheet in front of him. "Oh yes. Last week the membership promised to discuss the possibility of allowing random-bred dogs to participate in our show.

"I'm sure I know what the consensus of this group will be, but so we have it documented in the minutes that we lived up to our promise, I will now open the floor for discussion. Does anybody wish to speak?" He nodded toward the ruddy-faced man at the back of the room. "Go ahead, Arlo. You have the floor."

"Since Renee isn't here, I'd like to remind everyone of what she said last week. This show is for pedigreed animals. These mutts—okay, random-bred dogs—are anything but that. I think lettin' them show against our animals is a crazy idea."

"Duly noted," Wilbur said with an approving nod.

"I have to agree," Velma put in. "The whole notion of mixing purebred and mongrel dogs in the show ring is utterly ridiculous. We'd be the laughingstock of every dog club in the state. Maybe the nation, if word got around."

Kate cleared her throat and raised her hand.

Wilbur shot an irritated look in her direction. "Yes, Mrs. Hanlon?"

Kate rose to her feet and spoke clearly so everyone in the room could hear her. "I'd like to offer a different point of view. I think the idea of including all types of dogs has merit, whether they're purebred or random bred."

Wilbur glared at her, and Lucy Mae tapped her pencil on the tablet in front of her.

A veteran of countless church business meetings, Kate recognized a cold reception to an idea when she saw it. But all the years of participating in those meetings had taught her a thing or two about the art of persuasion.

She bestowed a smile upon each person present. "As members of this club, I'm sure a part of your mission is to educate the public about these wonderful animals and to build goodwill."

She heard a murmur of assent off to her left and took encouragement from that. "I'm sure you also want to foster an appreciation for dogs and to encourage people to become better dog owners."

Velma began to nod. "That's right. Of course we do."

Kate smiled her appreciation. "What better way to build goodwill than to include the owners of unpedigreed dogs in some of your activities rather than keeping them at arm's length as mere observers?"

Lucy Mae stopped her tapping and fixed her eyes on Kate, giving every indication of sincere interest.

Wilbur Dodson assessed the mood of the room with a glance. "What did you have in mind?"

"I'm not suggesting for one moment that you allow animals of random breeding to take part in your regular conformation classes"—she threw in a term she had picked up from her dog magazine—"but what about opening up a contest for a separate category of dog? Or you could have several classes if the interest warranted that."

Wilbur leaned forward and peered at Kate intently. "But how would we judge these new classes? We don't have any breeding standards for mongrels."

"Let's think creatively." Kate injected all the enthusiasm she could into her tone. "You could have a prize for the best-groomed dog, and one for the dog who does the best tricks. And what about a costume contest?"

She heard a quiet snicker behind her, but she kept on talking. She had built up too much momentum to quit now.

"Something that wouldn't take away from the prestige of your own competition, but would also allow the general public a chance to feel pride in their own dogs, even if they are unpedigreed."

To her surprise, a smattering of applause sounded around the room when she sat down.

Wilbur Dodson closed his eyes for a moment, then cleared his throat. Looking around the room, he asked, "Is there any further discussion?"

"Why not go along with her idea?" Arlo Sanders grinned.

"That makes a lot of sense. I move that we adopt Mrs. Hanlon's recommendation and that we do it for the good of the club. The public-relations value alone will be worth it."

"I second," called the woman sitting next to him.

"Very well, we'll put it to a vote. All in favor of Mrs. Hanlon's suggestion say *aye*."

A chorus of *ayes* rang out.

"Any opposed?"

No one spoke.

Wilbur looked mildly stunned but soldiered on. "Let it be noted that we will offer a contest for unpedigreed classes of dogs as stated. Is there any other business?"

Kate put her hand up again.

Wilbur eyed her with a haunted expression. "Yes, Mrs. Hanlon?"

"Just one more thought on the subject, if the club officers don't mind."

"You may proceed," Wilbur said, his face reddening.

"Thank you. In the spirit of fostering enthusiasm throughout the community and improving public relations, as Arlo pointed out, I would like to suggest creating some special awards that would be open to all dogs, pedigreed or not."

Wilbur frowned. "We already have ribbons and a Best in Show trophy. Mixed breeds would certainly not be eligible for those."

"That isn't the kind of award I mean," Kate said. "I was thinking about an Exhibitors' Choice Award that would be open to all dogs, whether they're of show quality or not."

That one got a smile from Lucy Mae.

The corners of Wilbur's lips pinched together. "Mrs. Hanlon, you must understand that this is a meeting of dog-club *members*. As a visitor—"

"And the head of our hospitality committee," Lucy Mae whispered forcefully. "A position which, may I remind you, was *very* difficult to fill . . ."

Wilbur sighed. "—your comments are much appreciated. Is there any discussion?"

Arlo chuckled. "In for a penny, in for a pound. I move we go along with the new awards too."

"Second," Velma said.

Wilbur Dodson rolled his eyes and bowed to the inevitable. "All in favor?"

"Aye!"

"Opposed?"

No one responded. "Fine," Wilbur said. "The motion passes. Since you are the one who initiated this, Mrs. Hanlon, I hereby delegate you to order these new awards. Put that in the minutes, Lucy Mae."

"I have one more question," Kate said. "Do you have any more information for me on what I'm supposed to be doing with regard to hospitality? I really haven't had much direction."

Wilbur's nostrils pinched. "It isn't difficult. Just greet the exhibitors as they arrive. Make sure the judges feel welcome and have everything they need. And be available to help the show committee or any of the exhibitors deal with minor problems that may arise. Matters of a more significant nature should, of course, be directed to me. Is that clear enough?"

It wasn't, but Kate nodded her head, knowing that was all she was likely to find out. "One more thing," she ventured. "Who else is on this committee I'm chairing? I need names so we can get together and make plans."

The corner of Wilbur's mouth twitched again. "The term *committee* may be something of a misnomer. Our shows are fairly small ones, and we haven't found it necessary to overstaff."

Kate's suspicions crystallized. "Are you saying—"

Wilbur nodded. "Mrs. Hanlon, you are the committee." He looked down at his agenda, then rapped on the table. "We have one more item to address, and then we're done for the day. The chair would like to ask the membership to authorize the purchase of a gavel."

The motion was made, seconded, and carried in a matter of seconds.

"Motion passed." Wilbur rapped on the table, then rubbed his knuckles. "And thank you very much. This meeting is adjourned."

When the meeting was over, Kate went in search of Livvy and found her at the front counter trying to resolve a dispute with a patron over a sizable overdue fine. Kate lingered a moment, then waggled her fingers in a silent farewell.

Livvy met her eyes over the perturbed man's shoulder and gave Kate a faint smile. They would have to talk another time.

Kate stepped outside and saw Kisses' likeness staring

back at her from a nearby lamppost. Her stomach tightened. The first batch of flyers had been up for four days
and had produced no results. Kate's thoughts drifted back
to Renee's remark about the importance of solving a kidnapping within the first forty-eight hours.

Surely someone knew what had happened to Kisses.
Why hadn't anyone called? Was the little Chihuahua all
right? Was he even in Copper Mill?

Kate watched as a long pink Oldsmobile turned onto
Main Street and came to a stop a few feet from where
Kate stood. She walked over to the car.

Renee lowered the passenger window, and Kate
leaned her arms on the edge. The diagram of Copper Mill
lay open on the seat usually occupied by Kisses.

"I know there was a meeting this morning," Renee said
in a crisp tone. "But I've been making my rounds, checking to make sure all the flyers are still in place. Anything
to report?"

Kate shook her head. "I'm afraid not. They spent most
of the time discussing the show. Wilbur and Lucy Mae are
still upstairs going over some last-minute details."

Renee sniffed and looked down the street. "I'm glad
they can go on with *their* lives. I'm sure everyone is
thrilled that my precious Kisses is out of the running for
the time being. Well, I suppose the show must go on." She
paused, and her shoulders sagged. "I really thought something would have turned up by now."

Kate felt a wave of sympathy for Renee, despite her
sarcastic remarks.

"I don't know what's gotten into people these days," said a voice even raspier than Renee's from the backseat of the Olds.

Kate leaned inside the car and nodded to Caroline, who was wearing one of her favorite flowered hats. Kate wondered how much of a struggle it was for the older woman to communicate with her daughter who was seated in the rear.

Kate spoke carefully. "I see you're keeping Kisses' seat vacant."

"Of course." Renee looked startled. "Doing otherwise would be like saying we've given up on finding him."

Her lips tightened. "I've been doing some research. It seems that dognapping is on the rise nationwide. Did you realize there are bands of professional thieves who specialize in stealing dogs? Sometimes they even sell them to foreigners and ship them out of the country!"

Kate had read a short article about the increase in dognappings in her new magazine, and it had only confirmed her suspicions that Kisses' disappearance wasn't an accident.

"But there are often happy endings as well."

Renee's optimism seemed forced to Kate.

"Yes, there are." Kate gave Renee a reassuring smile.

Renee blinked back tears and drew in a deep breath. "I must be on my way. I don't want to leave any stone unturned."

Kate stepped back and watched her drive away, then turned purposefully and strode back inside the library.

Seeing that Livvy was free again, she stepped up to the counter to talk to her friend.

"Would you like to do a little sleuthing for me?"

Livvy's eyes sparkled. "Sure, what do you need?"

Kate leaned over the counter and lowered her voice. "Renee is worried about the possibility of Kisses being stolen by professional dognappers. Is there any way you can check into that on the Internet?"

Livvy gave a quick nod. "I'll give it a shot. Any suggestions on where to start?"

"How about looking for Chihuahuas for sale in Tennessee? See if you can find anything that might indicate a notice that doesn't come from a legitimate breeder."

Livvy jotted a note on a slip of paper. "Okay, that'll give me enough to get started. Maybe I'll pick up on something along that way that will lead us in even more directions."

Kate smiled. "That's what I'm counting on."

She stepped back outside and headed toward her Honda. *Lord, I know you don't want us to worry, but I have to admit I'm very concerned for Renee. And Kisses, for that matter. Please help me find some answers so Renee can have a happy ending too.*

Chapter Eleven

After the worship service the following morning, people stood around and chatted in small clusters as usual. But instead of the typical discussions about the sermon or upcoming church events, the buzz was centered on the recent happenings around town.

Kate moved from group to group, smiling and greeting church members, pleased to see several who hadn't been to Faith Briar in a while. Strange how anything out of the norm often made people feel the need to reconnect with the Lord.

Near the rear of the sanctuary, Kate spotted a dark head and recognized Brenna Phillips. So Thursday's visit with Skip hadn't kept her from coming to church.

Kate waved to catch Brenna's eye and smiled. The girl only looked at her with a wounded expression and turned away.

Kate threaded her way through the crowd, but Brenna ducked out the door and was gone before she could reach her. Kate sighed and turned back toward the sanctuary.

Light streamed in through the stained-glass window at the front of the sanctuary, scattering shards of color across the pews and the floor.

Abby Pippins stepped over and looped her arm through Kate's. "Phoebe and I still can't get over how well things went at last week's Friendship Club meeting. We can't wait to see who shows up tomorrow. Will you be able to come?"

"I've been looking forward to it." Kate couldn't help but smile at the way Abby's whole face lit up. How could anyone say no to that kind of enthusiasm?

Abby squeezed Kate's arm and excused herself to go and extend an invitation to several retired ladies she spotted in a group on the opposite side of the room.

Kate continued to circulate through the congregation, this time paying more attention to the snatches of conversation she heard.

"What would anybody want with one of those little dogs, anyway?" Old Man Parsons wheezed. "I know Renee's crazy about him, but I don't take much stock in something so small you have to be careful where you're going to step."

A scrawny, gray-haired man standing beside Mr. Parsons snickered. "Maybe someone needed a lab animal and thought it was a rat."

Kate flinched and looked toward the front pews, hoping Renee hadn't heard. She saw Livvy talking to Renee and moved forward to join them. Before she reached Renee's pew, her attention was caught by another voice.

"I hear you had a close call over at your place the other day, Lester."

Kate stopped in the middle of the aisle, then moved over to join the group. The last time she had seen Skip, he'd been on his way to answer a call at the Philpott residence.

"That's right." Lester rubbed his hand across the top of his head. "I'd just gotten home from work. LeRoy and I were going to take my rottweiler, Maximillian, to a new groomer in Pine Ridge. She says she can groom him like nobody's business, but we wanted to see what she could do before we allow her to get him ready for the dog show. I heard a noise that sounded like somebody monkeyin' around in the carport, so I hollered and went out to see.

"Must have scared whoever it was away when I yelled. When I got out there, the prowler was gone."

"Do you think it was just your imagination?" Jeff Turner asked.

Lester shook his head. "When I started lookin' around, there was an open bag of sugar sitting next to my truck."

Jeff stared at him. "Do you think someone was going to pour it in the gas tank?"

"That's what it looked like to me." Lester's face was grim. "Don't know who would do somethin' like that."

"Whoa! Good thing you chased the culprit off first. That would have done a number on your engine."

Joe Tucker chimed in. "What in the world is going on? First, Renee's dog is stolen, then the Wilsons' house is TP'd. Now this. Toilet paper is one thing, but sugar in the gas tank—that's steppin' things up a notch."

Lester shook his head mournfully. "This is getting out of hand. I keep wondering who's going to be the next victim and what's going to happen to them."

A shiver ran up Kate's arms. *What, indeed?*

She glanced toward the front pews, where Livvy and Renee stood, deep in conversation. Kate hurried to join them.

"I was so sure the flyers Kate put up would have done the trick by now," Renee was saying. "But today's the fifth day they've been up. Wait until the *Chronicle* comes out next Thursday, though. I've taken out a half-page ad there, and in the Pine Ridge paper as well. That ought to get some action."

Livvy's eyes shone with sympathy. "I know this must be terribly difficult for you. If I can—"

"Oh, believe me, I already have a job for you."

Kate caught sight of a tag sticking up from the neck of Renee's patterned silk blouse. She reached over and tucked it in discreetly, knowing how embarrassed Renee would feel to have missed such a detail.

Renee tugged at her left earring—a plain gold hoop— in a nervous gesture, but didn't seem to realize that Kate was smoothing her blouse collar back in place.

"I want you to do some research on the Internet," she told Livvy. "You're much better at it than I am. If these villains are trying to sell my Little Umpkins, maybe you can find some trace of it online."

She turned her head, and Kate saw the silver earring dangling from Renee's right ear.

Kate's eyes met Livvy's, and she realized that her friend had noticed the mismatched earrings too. She knew the same thought must have been running through both their minds: only under extreme circumstances would Renee ever make such a fashion faux pas.

Livvy reached out and squeezed Renee's hand. "I'm already working on that. Kate asked me yesterday. I want to do anything I can to help bring Kisses home."

Kate opened her arms and enveloped both women in a hug. "That's what we all want."

KATE SPENT MONDAY MORNING in her studio working on several projects—a small lamp and three sun catchers she hoped to deliver to Smith Street Gifts later in the week.

A thunderstorm hit at noon, precluding the lunchtime walk she and Livvy often took. Paul had already told her he had a premarital counseling session with a young couple who could only come in during their lunch hour, so Kate made a simple tuna salad for her meal.

After cleaning up the kitchen, she pulled out the phone book and opened it to the pages listing numbers for Pine Ridge. Livvy was handling the Internet research, but a good sleuth didn't depend on a single source.

She ran her finger along the listings under D: Dixon . . . Dobbins . . . Dodson. There it was.

She repeated the number to herself while she punched it in on the kitchen phone. Renee had given her the impression that Wilbur Dodson was a retiree, but she

had no idea what he did with his time, or whether he
might be home during the day.

Kate listened to the soft *brrr . . . brrr . . . brrr . . .*
through the handset and was about to hang up when she
heard a pickup on the other end, followed by Wilbur's
voice saying, "Hello?"

"Mr. Dodson? This is Kate Hanlon. I'm glad I caught
you at home. Do you have time to talk? I have a few questions to ask you."

Wilbur clicked his tongue. "Really, Mrs. Hanlon, if
you have any other suggestions for the show, they will
have to be brought up at the next meeting."

Kate laughed. "I'm not trying to stir anything up this
time. I just needed to draw on your expertise as a knowl-
edgeable dog owner."

"Oh!" The relief in Wilbur's voice was obvious, even in
that short syllable. "That's a different matter, of course,"
he continued. "I'd be glad to help you. Were you thinking
of purchasing a pet for yourself?"

"No," Kate said quickly, then added, "at least, not at this
point. I'm just interested in gathering some information."

"I see." Wilbur's tone made it clear that he didn't.

"I'm looking for any information that might help me
locate Renee Lambert's dog, Kisses."

"A terrible thing, that. A tragedy for any dog owner. I'll be
glad to help, Mrs. Hanlon. What would you like to know?"

Kate paused a moment, trying to put her thoughts into
words. "There are people who buy and sell stolen property.
And I've heard that some people even sell stolen animals.

Do you think it's likely that Kisses may have been taken for resale?"

"Oh my, yes. Sad to say, there is a thriving black market for stolen dogs. The smaller breeds are particularly vulnerable to this."

"How much do you think a dognapper could expect to get on the black market?"

"It would be possible to get five hundred dollars or more, maybe even as much as four figures for a particularly desirable animal."

"But that would be for a dog with papers, wouldn't it?" Kate said. "How would they get around that?"

Wilbur gave a dry chuckle. "If someone is willing to go to criminal lengths to acquire a dog for illicit sale, do you really think a little thing like lack of documentation would stop them? Counterfeit documents are produced all the time, everything from passports down to—"

"Dog registration papers," Kate finished. "Of course. Thank you so much, Mr. Dodson. You've been a great help. Oh, one more thing. Do you know if one of these black-market operations is working in this area?"

"Unfortunately, they don't advertise." Wilbur's voice held a note of sarcasm. "But it's quite likely that there is, since the practice is so widespread. If I knew the people responsible for this, however, I would have picked up the phone and told them to return Renee's dog the moment he went missing."

"Of course." Kate felt thoroughly chastened. "Thank you again. I appreciate your help."

With time to spare before she needed to leave for the next Friendship Club meeting, Kate mulled over what she'd learned while she took out a dust cloth and some furniture polish and rubbed the oak dining table until the wood gleamed.

What if the motive for stealing Kisses had been purely one of profit, not a malicious act against Renee or an attempt to prevent Kisses from winning a trophy at the dog show?

Kate's arthritic knee twinged when she knelt down to apply the furniture polish to the legs of the table. Five hundred or even a thousand dollars wasn't a vast amount of money. But thefts had been committed for far less than that.

She pushed herself upright and carried the cleaning supplies to Paul's study, where she proceeded to polish his desk.

Then again, the concept of a large amount of money was relative. If someone was in desperate need of fifty dollars, five hundred would seem like a vast amount indeed.

But that would mean the person in dire need already had connections with an underground dog-theft ring. It wasn't the sort of thing a person could tap into by happenstance. As Wilbur Dodson said, the black market didn't advertise.

But since Kate hadn't heard about any other dog thefts in Copper Mill or the surrounding area, she thought it unlikely that a band of criminals was roaming the area in search of dognapping victims.

Kate put the cap back on the container of furniture polish, then returned the supplies to their places. Following the black-market theory hadn't been a bad idea, but it hadn't produced any likely leads either.

She returned to her studio to do just a bit more on her stained-glass projects before leaving for the meeting at Abby's. After a while, Kate looked at her watch and gasped when she realized that she had only a few minutes to get ready. She'd become so engrossed in her work that she'd completely lost track of the time.

With her hair neatly brushed and fresh lipstick applied, Kate grabbed her handbag and keys and started for the door. She hadn't gone five steps when the phone rang. Kate hurried to the kitchen, snatched up the receiver, and answered breathlessly.

"Are you sitting down, Kate?" Livvy's voice bubbled with excitement.

"I can't sit down. I'm on my way out the door to a Friendship Club meeting."

"Okay, I'll talk fast. You're never going to believe this. I was doing that Internet research Renee and you asked for . . ."

Kate's attention sharpened. She set her keys on the kitchen counter and concentrated on what Livvy was saying.

". . . and I started with a general search for Chihuahuas. Then I narrowed it down to people selling dogs of any kind in this area.

"There was lots of information," Livvy went on, "but

nothing that pertained directly to Kisses. I guess I got a little punchy after that and started typing in any keywords I could think of."

Kate glanced at her wristwatch and tapped the car keys on the counter. She didn't want to rush Livvy, but she would be late to the meeting if she didn't get out the door right away.

"So I typed in 'white designer totes' on a whim. And guess what I found?"

"What?"

"Would you believe, a listing for a white designer tote on eBay?"

Kate's interest flagged a notch. What could an online auction listing have to do with the missing Kisses?

She chose her words carefully. "Liv, there must be hundreds of those totes out there. To find one similar to Renee's—"

"It isn't just similar." The excitement in Livvy's voice practically bubbled over the phone line. "Think about it, Kate. This is eBay, where they have photos of the items that are up for sale. There are several shots of the tote on this page, and this one looks *exactly* like Renee's. She was showing it off to everyone in the library the day of the dog club meeting. You had already left for your hair appointment when she came downstairs. She was so proud of that tote; she showed me every detail."

Kate caught her breath, and a tingle of excitement rippled through her. "Oh, Livvy! What a find!" Then Kate let out a frustrated sigh. "I wish I could come to the library right this minute, but I have that meeting at Abby's."

"I know you've got to leave," Livvy said. "Can you meet me at the diner at five? I'll be off work by then. I'll print out a copy of the Web page and bring it with me."

"That's great, Livvy. I can't wait to see what you've turned up." Kate hung up the phone and made a beeline for the door.

She could barely contain her excitement. She wasn't sure she could stand a couple of hours of small talk when she knew that Livvy had information that could solve the mystery of Kisses' disappearance. But she'd waited this long for a break in the case. Livvy's find could keep a little longer.

Chapter Twelve

K ate managed to get to Abby's only a couple of minutes late. She had to park farther away from the house this time—a good sign, she decided, since that meant others were there already. The front door stood open, and she could hear the buzz of chatter before she reached the house.

Abby pushed the screen door open, her face flushed with pleasure.

"They came back!" she whispered. "I have to admit I was a little worried about it."

Kate looked around the room. Everyone she remembered from the first meeting was there, and she saw a sprinkling of new faces as well. She laughed and squeezed Abby's arm.

"What you and Phoebe are doing is connecting with a heartfelt need. I'm not at all surprised."

She laughed again. "I have a feeling the only thing you'll need to worry about is where to hold these meetings when this group outgrows your living room."

Abby's eyes shone. "Do you really think that might happen?" At Kate's nod, she beamed. "What a delightful

problem to have. Perhaps Phoebe and I should start praying about that right now, just in case."

"May I ask a question?" a voice called above the chatter.

"Of course," Abby said as the room quieted down.
"We're all ears."

One of the new visitors looked around shyly at the rest
of the women. "A lady down the street from me has a husband who's bedridden. They don't qualify for home health
care, so she has to stay with him all the time. I know she'd
love to get to know more people, but she can't leave the
house. So I was wondering . . . Why couldn't some of us
be her friends by going over and visiting with her? And
maybe we could take turns staying with her husband so she
can get out once in a while."

"That's a wonderful idea," said Patricia Harris. "When
my daughter was so sick, I found out how lonely it can feel
being shut off from everyone. Maybe we could clean her
house one day and take in some meals, just to give her a
break."

"That sounds like fun," Phoebe said. "Count me in."

"Me too," called several others.

"I know another woman who could use something like
that," Stephanie Miller added. "She's in a wheelchair and
says she gets tired of staring at nothing but the same four
walls every day. Why don't we make a list of people like
that and come up with ways we can help each one?"

"Love it!" Phoebe exclaimed.

The women began to discuss the idea in smaller
groups. Abby grinned at Kate, and Kate winked back at her.

Kate sidled up to Phoebe and reached over to smooth

back a lock of baby-fine hair from Violet's forehead. "She's getting more beautiful every day."

Phoebe grinned. "I won't argue with you, even though I guess I am a little biased."

"You're not biased." Patricia joined them. "She's one of the most beautiful babies I've ever seen."

Phoebe's eyes shone with maternal pride. "In that case, I—" She broke off, and a wide smile spread across her face. "Look who's here!" She hurried across the room to the front door.

Kate's lips parted in a smile, and she stared at the slim, dark-haired woman who knocked tentatively on the screen door.

"Welcome!" Phoebe pushed the door open and swept Lisa Phillips into the living room. "We're so glad you could make it."

"Oh my, yes." Abby bustled over to join them.

Kate lifted a silent prayer. *Thank You, Lord. You do work all things together for good!* Maybe the previous week's altercation had somehow awakened in Lisa a desire for connection with other women—and maybe someday with the Lord.

Lisa gave a shy smile that reminded Kate of Brenna's. She saw plenty of similarity between the two, from their dark hair and pixie features to their slim builds.

"I'm so happy to see her here," Patricia whispered to Kate.

Stephanie Miller leaned in. "Isn't her daughter the one the mayor's nephew has a crush on?"

"What?" Patricia grinned. "Young love in the making? I hadn't heard anything about that."

"That's what I heard," Stephanie said.

Kate couldn't help but be interested in this tidbit of information.

"He's actually Lucy Mae's nephew," Stephanie went on. "Apparently he's staying with them for the summer. Lawton told my husband the boy was driving his mom and his stepdad round the bend."

Kate's interest sharpened. Micah was so polite; he hadn't struck her as a troublemaker.

"What happened?" Patricia asked.

Stephanie shrugged. "Like a lot of kids his age, he got in with a bad crowd at his high school in Nashville. He didn't quite wind up on the wrong side of the law, but things were sure moving in that direction.

"That's why Lucy Mae invited him to stay here, so he could make a break from the old crowd over his summer vacation.

"And I'll tell you what. Lucy Mae dotes on that boy almost as much as she does on her dachshund." Stephanie chuckled.

Phoebe clapped her hands to get the group's attention and called out, "Everyone, I'd like you to welcome the newest member of our Friendship Club, Lisa Phillips."

The women responded with a chorus of welcome.

Lisa's shoulders lifted in a tiny shrug. "They changed my hours at work, and I got off early today. I thought I might as well drop by and see—"

Her words cut off abruptly the moment she saw Kate, and her features hardened. "What's *she* doing here?"

Half the women gaped at Lisa, and the other half stared at Kate.

With a shocked glance in Kate's direction, Phoebe sputtered, "It's a friendship club," as if that explained everything.

"That's right," Abby joined in. "Everyone's free to come."

"Then I guess that means I'm free to leave too."

Even from that distance, Kate could see Lisa's body tremble.

Abby laid her hand on Lisa's arm. "But she's a pastor's wife and our friend."

"All the more reason for me to go."

Kate crossed the room in a few quick steps and spoke in a low voice. "Lisa, please. It was all a misunderstanding. I never meant to imply—"

"Didn't you? Brenna likes the youth group at Faith Briar, but if this is the kind of thing I can expect from you people, maybe I should just pull her out."

Lisa's words seemed to hang in the air as she spun on her heel and headed out the door.

"Don't go." Kate caught up with Lisa on the front porch, with Abby and Phoebe close behind. "I'll leave instead. That way you can relax and enjoy yourself. I think you'll love the club, and everyone is so pleased to have you here. I don't want to get in the way of that. Why not give it a try?"

Lisa hesitated, and Phoebe seized the opportunity to

add her own plea. "Please stay. It's a wonderful group, and I just know you'll like getting to know everyone."

After a long, searching glance at Kate, Lisa nodded and followed Phoebe back inside.

Abby pressed her fingers against her cheeks. "Oh dear. I never expected anything like this."

Kate forced a smile and blinked to hold back the tears that stung her eyes. "It's all right, really. We all hoped Lisa would become a part of the group, and I'd rather step aside so she'll feel comfortable about being here."

"You don't mean you're going to quit coming entirely?" Abby caught Kate's hand in hers. "Don't make any hasty decisions. I appreciate you wanting to do what's best for Lisa, but let's make sure we do the right thing."

Kate nodded. "I just want to give her time to realize she's welcome without having to worry about me being here. In the meantime . . ."

"We'll pray about it," they both said at the same time.

Kate hugged Abby and made her way to her car, feeling more at peace about the situation. How blessed she and Paul were to live and minister among people who loved God and loved each other.

Paul was right. Her job was to keep on praying for Lisa and showing her the love of Christ. God would work in Lisa's heart in his own way and time.

Chapter Thirteen

With time on her hands due to her early exit from the meeting, Kate ran a couple of errands, then drove the few blocks to the diner and found Livvy in one of the back booths, sipping a tall glass of lemonade.

LuAnne bustled over and grinned at Kate. "What'll you have, darlin'? Lemonade or coffee?"

Kate slid into the booth and sighed. "How about a nice cup of chamomile tea?"

The lemonade looked wonderfully refreshing, but after Lisa's outburst at Abby's, she felt the need for something that would help steady her nerves.

LuAnne winked. "Got it." She headed off to the kitchen.

Livvy scooted forward. "You're here earlier than I expected. How did the meeting go?"

Kate wrinkled her nose. "I should have come straight over to the library instead of going to that meeting." She filled Livvy in on the altercation with Lisa Phillips.

"Wow." Livvy's eyes widened. "I'm so sorry, Kate. Try not to take it personally. I think you did the right thing by

offering to leave, though. And who knows what impact
that gesture will have on Lisa in the long run."

LuAnne returned with a steaming mug of tea and set
it on the table. "Here you go. Mind if I join you? We aren't
busy at the moment, and Livvy's got my curiosity all
stirred up."

"Sure. We can use all the help we can get." Kate
scooted over to make room for LuAnne. She stirred in a
spoonful of sugar, then took a sip and closed her eyes. Just
what she needed. The warmth of the tea combined with
Livvy's comforting words soothed her spirit.

"So, what's your opinion on this eBay listing Livvy
found?" she asked LuAnne.

The plump redhead snorted. "I don't have an opinion
yet. She said she wouldn't show me what she has until you
got here." She pointed a playful finger at Livvy. "Well,
we're all together now, so let's hear it."

Livvy's eyes twinkled. "Nothing like building suspense
to hold an audience." She pulled several sheets of paper
from her handbag and laid them on the table.

Kate recognized the brightly colored logo of the online
auction site. The listing included several photos of the
tote for sale. She studied them one at a time, passing each
one to LuAnne as she finished. Sure enough, the tote
looked identical to the one stolen from Rence.

The description read, "Elegant doggie tote combines
the look of a stylish handbag with comfort for the pet on
the go. Fine-leather exterior with zippered mesh top and
side panels."

"So, what do you think?" Livvy leaned across the table, barely able to control her elation.

"It looks like it," Kate conceded. "But as I said before, there must be dozens of others out there that look like this. And eBay sellers are everywhere. This could have been posted from anywhere in the country."

"Yes, but look." Livvy pointed at a line of print centered on the page. "Here, where it shows the item location, it says 'Deep South, USA.'"

Kate's pulse quickened. "Is there a way to contact the seller? We could ask where they're located and see what kind of response we get."

"Sure," Livvy said. "We just need to get back online and click on this link." She pointed to a link in blue print at the upper-right-hand corner of the listing. "That'll open up a window that will let us e-mail the seller directly."

"Why don't we go back to the library and do that right now?" Kate didn't want to put off following this lead any longer.

"Great idea!" Livvy reached for her glass. "Finish your tea, Kate, and let's go."

"Wait a sec. No need to go through all that." LuAnne's eyes remained fixed on the paper.

Livvy paused in the act of draining the last of her lemonade. "What do you mean? E-mailing sounds like a good idea to me."

"Look at this." LuAnne tapped her forefinger against the seller's screen name, *grannyardith*. "This isn't just somebody who's in the general region, gals. That's Ardith Bennett. She's right here in Copper Mill."

"Are you sure?" Kate said, her heart hammering.

"Sure as can be. She comes in here all the time, braggin' about the stuff she buys and sells on eBay. I always give her a hard time, but the woman's a pro."

Kate felt an electric tingle all the way down to her toes. Could it be possible that they might be able to locate Kisses and reunite him with Renee that very night?

"Do you know where she lives?" Kate asked.

"Yep. We can run out there right now, if you like."

"I'm game," Kate said. "I'll give Paul a quick call and let him know I won't be home to start supper for a while."

"Danny and the boys went fishing," Livvy said, "so I don't have to worry about supper for anybody but myself. Let's go."

"What's all the excitement?" said a raspy voice.

Kate jumped, then looked up to see Renee standing there. They had been so caught up in the thrill of learning that the eBay seller lived nearby, they hadn't noticed Renee approach. Her face looked drawn and pale under the fluorescent lights, and the corners of her mouth drooped downward.

"We may have a lead," Kate answered slowly, not wanting to get Renee's hopes up unnecessarily.

But as soon as the words were out of Kate's mouth, the older woman's eyes lit up. "You think you've found my Little Umpkins? Where is he? Tell me!"

Kate shook her head. "Not necessarily Kisses, but we may have located your tote."

Renee pressed her hand against the base of her throat. "But Kisses was in the tote. If you've found it—"

"We don't know that we've found it yet," Kate cautioned. "We're just going to go check something out. I'll call you as soon as—"

"You won't have to call me. I'll be right beside you."

"Now, Renee," LuAnne began.

Kate patted LuAnne's arm and shook her head. She knew Renee well enough to realize that attempts to dissuade her would be useless.

The three women scooted out of the booth and paid for their drinks. LuAnne took off her apron and told Loretta she was leaving, and then all four hurried out to Kate's Honda.

LuAnne pulled Kate aside while Livvy and Renee got into the backseat. "Are you sure it's a good idea for Renee to go along? She's a drama queen at the best of times, and this isn't one of them."

"I know," Kate whispered, "but think about it. Who would know better than Renee whether this tote is the right one? It's a good thing she's going along, really."

"I hope you're right about that. You've seen what she's like when she decides to pitch a fit."

Kate smiled at her friend. "That's why I'm glad I have you as backup. If she does explode, you'll be there to help me handle the situation."

LuAnne squared her shoulders and planted her hands on her broad hips. "I'll keep an eye on her. You can count on me."

The two women climbed into the Honda, and Kate started the car. The radio was tuned to a Harrington County oldies station, and Patsy Cline's voice warbling

"I Fall to Pieces" filled the car. Kate lowered the volume and followed LuAnne's directions to a home on Hamilton Road, not far from the park. She turned the motor off, and they sat staring at the house.

Kate felt a momentary twinge of doubt. Here they were, ready to accost a perfect stranger at dinnertime.

"How do you want to handle this?" LuAnne asked.

"You're the master sleuth around here, Kate," Livvy added, "so if you want us to hang back, we can do that."

Kate knew exactly what Livvy was hinting at. If Renee came along, anything could happen. "Well—" Kate looked at Renee.

"No way." Renee blurted. "If there's a chance of finding my Little Umpkins, I want to be in on this."

Livvy looked at Kate and gave her a rueful grin. "One for all and all for one, I guess. Lead on, Sherlock."

They piled out of Kate's car and walked up to the door. Kate knocked, smiling when she saw the way LuAnne and Livvy bracketed Renee who was off to her left.

A gray-haired woman holding a Yorkshire terrier opened the door and seemed taken aback at the sight of the four women clustered on her front porch.

She reached up to grip the edge of the door, as if she wanted to be sure she could shut it in a hurry. The tiny dog yapped at the strangers, and she shushed it gently. "Yes? May I help you?"

She looked over each of her visitors, her eyes lingering on Kate. "You're the pastor's wife at Faith Briar, aren't you? If this has something to do with trying to get me to come to your church, I'm already a member of First Baptist."

Out of the corner of her eye, Kate saw Renee open her mouth. But before the older woman could get a word in, Kate stepped forward. "No, this isn't church related. We're here about your online auction."

She held up the page Livvy had printed. "You did put this up on eBay, didn't you?"

The woman's pale blue eyes bulged when she saw the sheet in Kate's hand. "Yes, that's mine. But you're not supposed to contact a seller in person."

"We're not buyers," Kate said. "Not exactly, anyway."

"We just want to know where you got the tote, Ardith," LuAnne put in. "Is it one of those garage-sale things you're always pickin' up?"

Ardith put one plump hand on her hip in a gesture that reminded Kate of LuAnne. "I've had some strange requests before, but in all the time I've been selling online, I've never come up against anything like this."

She shook her head. "No, it didn't come from a garage sale. It's mine, and I have every right to sell it."

Renee stepped forward before LuAnne could stop her. "How long have you had it? I own one just like it that was stolen recently."

Ardith bristled. "Well, I didn't take it, if that's what you're implying."

Kate exchanged glances with Livvy, then jumped in before things got out of hand. "Please, we're not accusing you of anything. We thought perhaps you bought the tote somewhere, then decided to sell it. We were just hoping it might somehow be the same tote that was stolen along with Renee's little dog, Kisses."

That bit of news seemed to defuse the situation. Ardith's eyes gleamed with sympathy. "That's terrible. I don't know what I'd do if someone took my Little Honeymuffin." She cuddled the Yorkie and nuzzled the top of its head with her cheek.

Kate heard a sniffle beside her. She didn't dare look at Renee.

"I guess I can tell you about the tote," Ardith said. "My sister in Atlanta sent it to me as a birthday gift, but I just didn't like it."

"Didn't *like* it?" Renee burst out.

Ardith cast a nervous glance at Renee and shrugged. "It just isn't me. I didn't want to hurt my sister's feelings by asking her where to return it, so I thought I'd just sell it online and use the money to buy something I'd really like. Is that so wrong?" she asked defensively.

"Of course not," Livvy soothed, then she shot a relieved look at Kate.

"Just a minute." Apparently Renee wasn't ready to give up so easily. "May I see the tote?"

Ardith shrugged. "Sure. Hang on."

Leaving the door ajar, she retreated into the house.

As soon as Ardith had left, Renee addressed the group in a rasping whisper. "I'm not sure I buy that story. Why would anyone want to get rid of an expensive tote like that?"

Ardith returned with Honeymuffin trotting along at her feet. She held up the bag in one hand and a greeting card in the other. "This is the card from my sis. I hope that satisfies you."

Renee grabbed the tote and turned it over in her

hands. The manufacturer's tag was still looped around the handle. She pinched her lips together and held it up to show the rest of the group.

"All right, I can see that's brand-new. Someone trying to get rid of evidence wouldn't be able to put that tag back on."

Ardith glared at Renee and sniffed indignantly. "It's mine, no doubt about it."

"Thank you very much," Kate said. "We're sorry to have bothered you. I hope we didn't interrupt your supper."

Ardith's genial smile returned. "Not to worry. I was just going to pop a TV dinner in the microwave. I've got an auction ending in twenty minutes, and I want to be in front of my computer to watch the last-minute action."

She started to swing the door closed then pulled it open again. "By the way, I haven't had any bids on that tote yet. I don't suppose you want to buy this one to replace the one that was stolen?"

Kate saw Renee's stricken expression and hurried to say, "Not now. But thanks for the offer. We'll keep it in mind."

"Well, that was a bust," LuAnne said on the way back to the diner.

Livvy sighed. "I so hoped it might prove to be something helpful."

"Don't feel bad," Kate said. "It was a good lead, and it was worth—"

"Hush!" Renee snapped.

Kate stared at Renee's reflection in the rearview mirror. "Excuse me?"

"Turn up your radio!"

"What in the world?" Kate murmured but did as she was told.

The announcer's voice crackled through the speakers. ". . . missing from the Copper Mill area. The dog was wearing a jeweled collar. Answers to the name Kisses. The dog's owner is offering a reward for her Little . . . Umpkins?"

The announcer cleared his throat and continued. "The owner would also like to make the public aware that a dognapping ring may be at work in the area and begs all pet owners to keep their . . . precious . . . animals safe."

Dead air followed for a few beats before the announcer went on. "In other local news . . ."

"You can turn it down now." Renee's voice held a satisfied note. "That should get some response, don't you think? I talked to the station manager this morning. They're going to run the announcement at regular intervals until Kisses is found. Between the radio spots and my newspaper ads, everyone in the county should be on the lookout for him."

Chapter Fourteen

Trust in the Lord with all your heart and lean not on your own understanding; in all your ways acknowledge him, and he will make your paths straight.

Kate laid her Bible in her lap and took a long sip of coffee. She leaned back in her rocking chair and studied the cup in her hand. She had purchased the delicate china cup from Eli Weston on a whim during one of her visits to Weston's Antiques.

Kate traced her finger around the gold-edged rim, admiring the delicate floral design that formed scallops along the upper edge. She had often wondered if she loved antiques because they spoke to her of a time when life was less hectic. She took another sip and set the cup on its matching saucer with a soft click.

Closing her eyes, Kate rested her head against the back of the rocker. A less hectic pace was just what she needed after the events of the previous day.

"Lord," she breathed, "I need you to make my path straight right now. I don't know where to turn next."

Her eyes flew open. Or did she? Something she had heard the day before had been dancing on the edges of her mind, but between the altercation with Lisa Phillips and checking out Livvy's lead on the tote, her mind hadn't been clear enough to focus on it.

Brenna had admitted to being on the bridge the day Kisses was stolen, but she had refused to give them any other information. She'd insisted that it had nothing to do with the case, but Kate wondered if there might be some connection Brenna didn't know about.

Kate closed her eyes again and thought, trying to remember exactly what Brenna had said and what she'd heard from Stephanie Miller in Abby Pippins' living room. She felt certain she was holding several pieces of the puzzle in her hands, but she didn't know how they all fit together.

By midmorning, the breakfast dishes were washed and put away, and Kate had some salmon steaks marinating in the refrigerator for their supper that night.

Kate's thoughts returned to Brenna. Even on a hot summer day, the ice-cream shop wouldn't be busy in the morning. It was a perfect opportunity for the two of them to have a little talk. Kate grabbed her keys and headed out the door.

"HI THERE, KATE!" Emma Blount called when Kate stepped inside. The shop's owner jutted her chin to indicate the large cardboard box she held in her chubby arms. "I wish I had time to chat, but a new order of cups and cones just came in, and I've got half a dozen boxes to sort through while Brenna mans the counter."

"No problem. I'm sure Brenna can take care of me."

The dark-haired girl behind the counter gave Kate a tentative smile but eyed her warily. Kate couldn't blame her after their last encounter.

"What would you like, Mrs. Hanlon?"

"Two cones, please. Make the first one a double scoop of mint chocolate chip."

Brenna wielded the ice-cream scoop with ease and handed the cone to Kate. She reached for another cone. "What about the second one?"

"A double scoop of anything you'd like. My treat." Kate smiled at the look of surprise on Brenna's face. "Consider it a peace offering for stirring things up at your house the other day."

Brenna hesitated a moment, then grinned. She dipped the scoop in a container of water and served herself a combination cone of triple fudge and chocolate ripple. She rang up the order, accepted Kate's payment, and slipped the money into the register. "Thanks, Mrs. Hanlon."

"You're welcome. Do you think we could chat for a few minutes?"

Brenna looked around the otherwise empty shop and shrugged. "Might as well." She grabbed a handful of napkins and chose a seat at one of the round tables.

"Are you going to keep working here after school starts up again?"

Brenna bit into the scoop of chocolate ripple. "*Mmm.* You'd think I'd get tired of ice cream from working here, but it hasn't happened so far. Uh, I'm not sure what I'll be doing once school starts. My mom isn't convinced I can keep my grades up and work too."

Kate sampled her mint chocolate chip and gave a happy sigh. "I see what you mean. I don't think I'd get tired of this either." She tilted her head to take another lick of ice cream and observed Brenna from under her lashes. "You said the other day you wanted a job to prove to your mom that you're responsible?"

"Yeah." Brenna paused to lick an errant drip of triple fudge that had made its way down the side of her cone. She spent a few more seconds swirling the cone against her tongue to pick up any other stray drips. "I've been wanting a dog for ages, but my mom said no."

Kate felt a shiver of excitement, but she kept her voice steady. "Your mother doesn't like dogs?"

"It isn't that. She said we couldn't afford one. I thought if I got a job, she'd see I could make enough money to take care of the food and shots and license—all that sort of thing—and she might change her mind."

Kate sensed that she might be onto something, but she reminded herself to tread with caution. She finished the top scoop of mint chocolate chip and started on the second scoop. "Do you have any particular type of dog in mind?"

Brenna shook her head. "Not really. I like big dogs, but Mom says we don't have enough room for one. Besides, I don't know if I can make enough money to feed a big one. Maybe I'd better go with something smaller."

She looked around the shop. "This is a good place to

talk to people about it. When I find out a customer has a dog, I try to ask a few questions and see what they suggest. Everybody always seems happy to talk about their pets."

Kate smiled. "Like the mayor's nephew?"

Brenna's face brightened, then took on a mask of indifference. "Yeah, his aunt has that little dachshund. Micah seems to like it."

"Lucy Mae introduced him to me the other day." Kate nibbled the edge of her cone. "He seems like a nice boy."

"He's okay."

After raising three kids of her own, Kate recognized the overly casual tone. Micah wasn't the only one who had a crush. "Do you see much of him, or does your job keep you too busy?"

"I only work three days a week, so we can get together pretty often."

Kate blotted her lips with a napkin, then crumpled it in her hand. She squeezed it tight while she asked gently, "Was it Micah who was on the bridge with you?"

A light flush tinted Brenna's cheeks, and she looked down at the table. "Yeah. I guess it doesn't matter if I tell you now. The bridge is a good place to talk without anybody seeing us. My mom doesn't think I'm ready for a boyfriend yet."

Kate knew all too well the kinds of things a love-struck adolescent boy might do to win the favor of a girl he liked. And Micah must have known that Brenna had her heart set on owning a dog.

She took a deep breath and leaned forward. "Brenna, I have to ask you this. Did Micah take Kisses so he could give him to you as a gift?"

Brenna shook her head emphatically. "No, that would be an awful thing to do! I know how much that little dog means to Mrs. Lambert."

Kate settled back but kept her eyes fixed on the girl's face. "So it wasn't Renee Lambert's bag I saw fall into the creek?"

"No! I told you I didn't have anything to do with that. Micah didn't either."

Kate felt reasonably certain that Brenna was telling the truth, but she didn't want any more unanswered questions to come back and haunt her later. "Then what did you and Micah throw off the bridge?"

Brenna's eyes took on a shuttered expression, and she scraped her chair back. "I have to get back to work. Thanks for the ice cream." She tossed the last of her cone into the trash and went back behind the counter, studiously ignoring Kate's gaze.

PAUL HUNG UP THE PHONE and crossed the last name off his list. Years before, when he became the assistant pastor at Riverbend Community Church in San Antonio, he'd developed the habit of contacting members of his congregation on special occasions like birthdays and anniversaries. He'd continued the practice even after he became the senior pastor.

Over time, Riverbend grew to a size that made it

impossible for him to stay in touch with each member that way. Now that he was back in a small church setting, he embraced the opportunity to enjoy that kind of personal connection again.

He glanced at the clock on his office wall. Almost time to leave for lunch. He straightened the papers on his desk and pushed them into the upper-left-hand corner.

A quick rap on his office door was followed by Millie stepping inside. "Lisa Phillips just phoned," she began without preamble.

Paul tented his fingers and waited. There was no point in trying to hurry Millie. She would get around to giving him the details in her own good time.

"That car of hers has broken down again. She said it makes a terrible grinding noise when she turns the key in the ignition. She thinks it might be the starter."

Paul shook his head. At the rate Lisa was purchasing new parts for the rundown vehicle, she would have enough to build a new car from scratch before long.

"She can get something for lunch there in Pine Ridge," Millie went on, "but she won't be able to get home after work unless someone comes up and fixes the car or gives her a ride. She was wondering if she could get some help from the car-care clinic."

Millie sniffed. "I don't know why she keeps putting up with that old rattletrap. It's nothing but trouble."

Paul pushed back his chair and stood, ignoring her comment. "No problem. I can grab a quick sandwich at home and run up to Pine Ridge myself."

"Lisa said she didn't want you."

Paul's mouth dropped open. "What?"

Millie folded her arms and shook her head. "She was talking so fast, I couldn't hear everything she said, but I did catch her saying something about 'that woman.'" She arched her eyebrows. "I suppose that means your wife. I heard they had some kind of blowup the other day."

Paul let out his breath in a long sigh and sat down again. "Well, I wouldn't call it a blowup. It was just a misunderstanding."

He drummed his fingers on the desktop and looked up at the scowling woman. "I know you're ready to leave, so I'll take care of it from here, Millie. Thanks for passing the message along."

Millie huffed and closed the door behind her.

Paul sat deep in thought. He wondered if Lisa would have talked to him directly if he'd been available to take her call. Given the way she felt about what happened between her and Kate, it must have taken a lot for her to make the call in the first place. But it didn't seem she had anywhere else to turn.

Millie was right, a new car would be the answer. But if Lisa didn't have the funds to keep this one maintained, she sure didn't have the money to buy a replacement vehicle.

He sat a moment longer, weighing his options. Carl, the obvious choice to deal with this, was in Chattanooga for the day, attending a training session to sharpen his mechanical skills. Eli wasn't a lot better than Paul when it came to diagnosing problems.

That left Jeff Turner, who had shown great mechanical

aptitude, though he wasn't a mechanic by trade. At least his abilities were far above Paul's and Eli's.

Paul picked up the phone and dialed Jeff's cell number. Jeff answered a moment later.

"Hey there, Jeff. It's Paul. Sorry to bother you at work."

"It's okay. I'm on my lunch break. What's up?"

Paul explained Lisa's situation. "It may just be the starter, or it could turn out to be something else altogether. For some reason, she'd prefer that I wasn't involved. Would you mind going up there and taking a look at it?"

"Sure. I'd be glad to do it, as long as she doesn't mind waiting until I get off work." Jeff didn't ask why Paul wasn't welcome.

"I'm sure she won't. I think she'll be relieved to know she'll be able to get home tonight. Let me give you her number at work." He pulled the phone directory from his desk drawer, looked up the listing for Fancy Fabrics, and read the number off to Jeff.

"If you'd just give her a call and let her know you'll be there to bail her out, I think it would ease her mind."

"No problem. Consider it done."

"Thanks, Jeff. I appreciate it. Let me know how it all turns out, okay?"

Chapter Fifteen

"What do you have planned for this afternoon, honey?" Paul asked Kate on Thursday as he helped her clear away the lunch dishes.

"Well, the lamp and sun catchers I've been working on are ready to go, so I thought I'd drop them off at Smith Street Gifts. And I need to stop at Betty's to pick up some new conditioner she talked me into ordering. It's supposed to give my hair a youthful sheen."

She fluffed her strawberry-blonde curls. "At least part of me will look young."

Paul wrapped his arms around her and pulled her close. "Katie girl, to me you'll always be the beautiful young woman I met in San Antonio."

Kate looked up at him and laughed. "And you'll always be that athletic new minister who first caught my eye."

Paul struck a Charles Atlas pose. "You're not saying I'm a ninety-seven-pound weakling now, are you?"

Kate reached up to squeeze his biceps and batted her eyes at him. "Ooh, what big muscles you have. Why don't you put them to good use and go load those stained-glass pieces into the car for me while I wash the dishes?"

Paul bowed with a flourish. "Your wish is my command."

He started out of the room, then turned back, a more serious expression on his face. "By the way, I've been putting off telling you, but you probably ought to know that Lisa Phillips called the church a couple days ago, asking for help with her car."

"I don't get it . . ." Kate drew her eyebrows together. "If she's willing to talk to us again, that should be good news, right? So why put off telling me?"

"That wasn't exactly what happened. She wanted the help, but she made it clear she didn't want it from me."

Kate's playful mood evaporated. "Because of me," she whispered.

Paul closed the distance between them and pulled her into another hug. "I knew it would make you feel bad. That's why I haven't said anything. But I knew you'd feel even worse if you found out later and hadn't been able to pray about it."

"You're right about that." Kate gave him a grateful squeeze, then looked into his eyes. "I may not know how to fix this, but I know who does."

COOL, REFRESHING AIR washed over Kate when she stepped inside the beauty parlor. Lucy Mae Briddle sat across from Betty at the small manicure table near the back. Martha Sinclair sat up front in one of the salmon-colored chairs, having her hair styled by Ronda.

Betty looked up and smiled. "Hi, Kate. I'll be right with you." She touched one of Lucy Mae's fingernails gently. "Okay, you're good to go."

Kate waited while Lucy Mae reached into her purse and gingerly fished out a bill, which she handed to Betty.

Betty tucked the money in the pocket of her smock. "You're here for that conditioner, right?" She walked over to a small set of shelves and retrieved a cream-colored plastic bottle. "My sales rep swears by this stuff. Says it'll—"

The door burst open, and a wild-eyed woman rushed inside. Kate stepped back in time to keep from being run over.

Betty stopped in her tracks and stared. "Why, Maribeth, what's wrong?"

The frantic woman darted over to Betty. "It's an emergency. You've got to help me."

Kate exchanged a glance with Lucy Mae, who looked every bit as mystified as Kate felt. Martha and Ronda were frozen like statues, wearing identical expressions of shock.

"I will if I can," Betty said. "But what on earth's the matter?"

Maribeth wrung her hands and moaned. "It's Mitzi," she wailed.

"Your little Pomeranian?" Betty shook her head. "Hon, if you have a dog emergency, you need to see the vet, not me."

"You don't understand," Maribeth sobbed. "Someone

snuck into my backyard and . . . and . . . wait a minute, I'll show you. She's out in the car. It's horrible!"

She dashed back out the door as quickly as she had come in. The five women in the shop stared at each other.

Betty looked at the others and raised her hands. "Does this sound a little peculiar to anyone else but me?"

Before any of them could say a word, Maribeth rushed back inside carrying what looked like a pile of shaggy, blue carpet. Then the rug moved, and Kate realized she was looking at a dog.

The little animal seemed to share none of its owner's distress. Bright black eyes glinted with good humor from the depths of the sky blue fur.

Kate stepped forward and took a closer look. Even close up, the blue bundle looked more like a huge ball of cotton candy. Or like Cookie Monster wagging a plumed tail.

"Look!" Maribeth sobbed. "See what they did to my poor baby?"

Everyone in the room seemed too shocked to speak. Lucy Mae took a step nearer, her eyes wide, and simply stared.

"How did they do it?" Martha finally asked.

"I don't know," Maribeth wailed. "My husband thought maybe they sprayed blue food coloring over her."

"It might have been blueberry juice," Martha offered helpfully.

Betty leaned over and rubbed Mitzi's fur between her fingers, then leaned down to sniff her coat. "I honestly can't tell you what it is. There just isn't any way for me to know for sure. The best-case scenario is that it's some of that temporary hair color the kids use."

"Temporary?" Maribeth's face lit up as if Betty had thrown her a lifeline.

"Sure. If that's what it is, it'll wash out eventually."

"You mean we'll be able to get it out in time for the dog show two weeks from Saturday?"

Betty shook her head. "Even the temporary stuff doesn't wash out that fast. It takes some time, and that's on human hair. I have no idea how it'll react to a dog's coat, since it's more porous. And with all that white fur . . ."

Maribeth's shoulders shook. "*Blue* fur, you mean."

Lucy Mae reached out and touched the dog's sky blue coat with tentative fingers. Then she stepped back and slung her purse strap over her shoulder. "I've got to run. I'm so sorry about your dog, Maribeth. I do hope you figure out some way to get her ready for the show."

Kate watched Lucy Mae as she left the shop, then turned back to the unfolding drama.

"Who do you think did it?" Martha asked.

"Anybody could have." Maribeth mopped at her tear-stained face with her free hand. "Mitzi stays in the backyard when I'm not home. Anyone could have climbed over our fence and gotten to her. She might bark once or twice, but that's just her way of saying hello. She wouldn't harm a soul."

Her eyes misted over again. "Mitzi loves to go to the groomer's. She probably thought whoever did this was giving her some kind of beauty treatment."

Betty looked over at Kate and blinked. "Oh yeah. Your conditioner." She glanced down at the bottle in her hand and shook her head. "Here you go. Sorry, I got sidetracked."

"Totally understandable." Kate gave Betty a sympathetic smile and paid for her new product.

"Do you think peroxide might work?" It appeared that Maribeth wasn't willing to give up hope just yet.

Kate didn't wait to hear Betty's reply. She needed to get away by herself and think. She drove west on Main and turned right onto Smith Street, where she found a parking spot across the street from the gift shop.

Farther down the block, she spotted the mayor's Buick parked in front of the Country Diner. Acting on impulse, Kate walked to the other end of the block and entered the diner. Lucy Mae, Lawton, and Micah were sitting at a table for four.

"Afternoon, Kate," Lawton called. "We decided to stop in here for a piece of pie. Care to join us? We've only just ordered."

"I'd love to," Kate said. "But I think I'll just have a glass of iced tea."

LuAnne had the plates of pie on the table in no time, then brought Kate's iced tea.

Kate spread her napkin on her lap. "I wonder if I could ask a favor? Would you mind if I borrowed Micah for a few minutes after we're finished here? I need to carry some stained-glass pieces into Smith Street Gifts, and I could use some extra muscle."

Lucy Mae looked startled, then smiled. "It's all right with me if it's all right with Micah."

Micah shrugged. "Yeah, sure."

Kate smiled her thanks, then added in a casual tone, "It's a shame about Maribeth's dog, isn't it?"

Lucy Mae only nodded.

Lawton frowned. "What are you talking about? Has another dog been stolen?"

"Not stolen. Somebody sneaked into her backyard and dyed her Pomeranian blue." Kate sipped her tea and watched Lucy Mae over the rim of her glass.

Lucy Mae stared at her plate as if fascinated by her slice of peach pie.

"We've had a rash of vandalism lately," Lawton said in his most official tone. "I'm looking into it. I won't stand for this kind of thing going on in my town."

"That's good," Kate said. "It would be nice if nothing like this happened again."

"A lot of it seems to have to do with dogs too," Lawton said. "Seems like this dog show is turning the whole town upside down. I should have put my foot down and kept them from holding it here in the first place."

When Lawton finished his last bite, and his diatribe, Lucy Mae wadded her napkin on the table and pushed back her chair. "I need to get home and check on Sir Percival. I've left him too long already."

The others stood up too, and Lawton rolled his eyes at Kate. "Dogs, dogs, dogs."

Kate laid cash for her iced tea on the table and followed them to the door. "You don't need to wait for Micah," she told the Briddles. "I can drop him off at your house when we're finished."

"Oh, that's okay," Micah said. "I thought maybe I'd hang around downtown awhile."

"He likes it here." Lawton beamed proudly. He patted Micah's shoulder. "All right, we'll see you later. You can just walk home whenever you're ready. Nice talkin' to you, Kate."

Kate led Micah down to the end of the block and crossed the street. When they reached her car, she leaned back against the side and put her hands in her pockets.

Micah hovered beside her, looking confused. "Where's the stuff you want me to help you carry?"

"Oh, it's in the trunk. Thanks for being willing to help me unload these pieces, Micah. But before we carry them in, I wanted to give you the opportunity to unload something else first. Have you ever heard of the old expression that confession is good for the soul?"

Micah took a step backward, and his brows drew together. "What are you talking about?"

Kate studied him intently. "Micah, I'm just going to come out and say this: you're the one who dyed Maribeth's Pomeranian blue, aren't you?"

"Me? Why would you think—"

"I saw your aunt's face in the beauty shop when they were talking about someone using a temporary color on the dog. She left immediately afterward, and she was very uncomfortable when I brought the subject up again at the diner."

"Well, that doesn't mean . . ."

Kate waited for the boy to continue, but he seemed to

be wrestling with his conscience. He braved it out a moment longer, then wilted. "Okay, you're right. I did it."

"And the toilet paper on Carl Wilson's house?"

Micah's shoulders slumped, and he traced an arc on the sidewalk with the toe of his sneaker. "Yeah, that was me too."

"And the sugar at the house with the rottweiler," he added, as if relieved to unburden himself completely.

Kate spread her hands wide. "But why? You seem like such a nice young man. Why on earth would you do such malicious things?"

"None of it hurt anybody," he mumbled.

Kate raised her eyebrows. "What about the fact that Maribeth can't show her dog now? And do you know how much damage it would have done if you'd managed to pour the sugar into the gas tank of Lester Philpott's truck?"

"I wasn't actually going to put it in the gas tank. I just wanted him to think someone was after him."

"This makes absolutely no sense to me at all." Kate shook her head. "Do your aunt and uncle have any idea you were behind all the vandalism?"

"No. At least, I don't think so. You're probably right about Aunt Lucy Mae having a pretty good idea about the blue dye, but I don't want her to know about the other stuff. You're not going to tell them, are you?"

"I can't promise that, but we'll see. First, why don't you tell me why you did it?"

Micah swallowed. "I was doing it for my aunt."

"For your aunt?" Kate gestured toward a bench on the edge of the Town Green. "Let's go over there and sit down. I have a feeling there's quite a story behind all this."

Kate settled herself on the bench and waited until Micah joined her. "So, what's all this about your aunt? Are you mad at her? Wanting to get back at her for some reason? Has she asked you to do these things?"

"No, that isn't it at all. She wants to win that dog show so bad, and I was just trying to help her. She had nothing to do with it."

"Okay." Kate drew the word out. "So draping the Wilsons' yard in toilet paper and putting sugar next to Lester's pickup was going to accomplish this . . . how?"

Micah slumped on the bench, looking as if he wished he could disappear in a puff of smoke.

"I really like my aunt, okay? I wouldn't do anything to hurt her. Here's the deal. My parents got divorced when I was just a little kid. It was just me and my mom, and she had trouble taking care of me on her own. So Aunt Lucy Mae invited me to come live with her and Uncle Lawton.

"I stayed with them until I was in fourth grade, when my mom got married again. My aunt helped me with my homework and bought me clothes and took me to Boy Scouts . . . Everything a real mom is supposed to do."

The strain in his voice tugged at Kate's heartstrings.

"I don't know what would have happened to me if it hadn't been for Aunt Lucy Mae."

"Okay," Kate said slowly. "But that doesn't explain all the mischief."

Micah took in a quick breath of air and let it out in a huff. "I didn't want to do anything to hurt the other dogs, but I know how much my aunt has been fussing over getting ready for the show. I just thought if their owners got rattled enough, it would give her a little bit of an edge."

Kate's voice was gentle when she said, "Micah, didn't you come back to stay with your aunt this summer because you were having some problems back home? How do you think it's going to help your aunt if you get into trouble here?"

The boy slammed the palm of his hand against the bench. "You're right, it was a dumb thing to do."

"Well, we can agree on that point. Do you have plans for any of the other dogs around Copper Mill?"

"No." One corner of Micah's lips lifted. "Well, I did have a couple of ideas, but I guess I'm not going to follow through on them now."

"I should hope not. Now I have one more thing to ask you, and it's very important that you tell me the truth." Kate leaned forward and fixed her eyes on his. "Did you have anything to do with taking Renee Lambert's Chihuahua?"

Micah scooted back on the bench and looked at her with a wounded expression. "No. I wouldn't go that far, even for my aunt."

Kate studied him for a long moment, then said, "All right. Then I'll make you a deal."

Micah looked at her questioningly.

"I won't say anything to your aunt and uncle about what you've just told me, *if*"—she held up a warning finger—"you promise me nothing like this will ever happen again. And I'll be watching, you can be sure of that. If I get even a hint that you've been up to more mischief, the deal is off."

The boy nodded eagerly. "You've got yourself a deal."

"Good." Kate stood up and dusted off her slacks. "Now, let's get those stained-glass pieces over to the gift shop."

After the lamp and sun catchers had been delivered, she pulled a couple of dollars from her purse and handed them to Micah.

"What's this for? You don't have to pay me."

"I know I don't." Kate pressed the money into his hand. "But I appreciate your help . . . and our talk. Now, why don't you go buy yourself a cone over at Emma's Ice Cream?"

Micah's gaze flickered to one side, then he looked down at the sidewalk. "I'm not sure that'd be such a good idea."

"Go ahead," Kate urged with a smile. "You deserve a treat after helping me . . . and there's a young lady there who I think would like very much to see you."

Chapter Sixteen

After dinner that evening, Paul went to shower and change before the men's prayer meeting.

Kate headed for the kitchen. She needed some fresh ideas for finding Kisses, but inspiration seemed to elude her. It was time to fall back on her tried-and-true method for working through a puzzle. She leafed through her recipes, looking for a summertime favorite.

She pulled out a recipe for chocolate-fudge oatmeal cookies, a no-bake treat her kids had clamored for during their growing-up years. She combined sugar, milk, cocoa, and butter in a saucepan, then stirred the mixture carefully while she brought it to a boil.

There had to be some way to find Kisses, some clue she had overlooked. She removed the saucepan from the burner, then stirred in vanilla extract and chopped pecans. The little dog couldn't have just vanished off the face of the earth!

She added oatmeal and a handful of chocolate chips to the mixture, then blended the ingredients together.

Deftly, she began to form the stiff dough into balls the size of small walnuts and placed them evenly onto baking sheets lined with waxed paper.

The doorbell rang as Kate was sliding the first sheet into the refrigerator, and she jumped.

"Want me to get that?" Paul stepped into the kitchen, looking fresh and quite handsome in khaki-colored Dockers and a pale blue polo shirt that brought out the vivid blue of his eyes.

"Would you, please? My hands are all gooey."

Kate reached for another pan, then began rolling out the rest of the cookies. She heard the front door open and recognized Jeff Turner's voice.

"Come on back to the kitchen," Paul said. "Kate's in the middle of one of her baking projects."

"Hi, Kate." Jeff leaned on the counter and eyed the chocolate-chip-studded dough balls on her baking sheet. "Those aren't the chocolate-fudge-oatmeal kind, are they?"

Kate looked up from arranging the cookies on the waxed paper and laughed at his hopeful expression. "I've heard of people having educated palates. You, apparently, have an educated eye."

"My mom used to make them. They were my favorite." Deep lines creased Jeff's tanned cheeks when he smiled.

Kate could take a hint. "The first round just went into the fridge. Give them a few more minutes, and then you can sample some."

Jeff's face brightened even more. He turned to face Paul, resting one elbow on the counter. "I wanted to let you know I got Lisa Phillips' car up and running again."

Kate flinched, remembering Lisa's refusal to let Paul be involved in helping her.

"Glad to hear it," Paul said. "Did it turn out to be more complicated than we expected?"

"No, it was just the starter, but the auto-parts store in Pine Ridge didn't stock the one she needed. They had to order one from Chattanooga. I'd taken my tow dolly along, just in case, so I just attached it to the back of my truck and towed her car home."

Paul's forehead furrowed. "That's a shame. Did Lisa have to miss a day of work yesterday?"

Jeff gave a short laugh. "No. I took her to work in the morning and picked her up at the end of the day. The parts store got the starter in their afternoon shipment, so I brought it over to her place last night and put it on for her."

Paul clapped the younger man on the shoulder. "Wow. That's a lot of work, Jeff. I really appreciate it. I didn't expect you would have go to those lengths when I asked you to look into it the other afternoon."

"No problem." Jeff's grin looked a little sheepish. "Lisa and I talked a lot in the truck, and last night she sat out in the carport and chatted with me while I worked on her car."

Paul raised his eyebrows. "Oh, really?"

A dull, red flush rose above the collar of Jeff's shirt and spread up his neck. Kate turned to hide a smile and busied herself putting the second baking sheet into the refrigerator. Then she took the first batch out and set some of the cookies on three small plates.

She recognized the signs. She'd seen that look on her son Andrew's face when he first became interested in his wife, Rachel. Kate set the plates on the counter.

"It's funny," Jeff said. "I have to admit I wasn't looking forward to the drive home that first night. She's always seemed so reserved when she's come to the car clinic. Kind of on edge, if you know what I mean."

Paul nodded. "I've noticed that."

Jeff picked up one of the cookies off his plate. "But she really opened up when it was just the two of us." He bit into the cookie, and an expression of pleasure spread across his face. "Wow!"

Kate tilted her head. "I take it they're okay?"

Jeff took another bite and smiled around the mouthful of cookie. He finished chewing, then said, "I'd never tell my mom this, but these are even better than the ones she made."

Kate poured glasses of cold milk and set them on the counter. "Wouldn't we be more comfortable at the kitchen table?"

Paul glanced at his watch. "Sorry. I'd like to stay around and chat, but I really don't have time. The men's prayer meeting starts soon."

Jeff washed down his cookie with a long gulp of milk before he spoke. "I didn't mean to hold you up. I'm actually coming to the prayer meeting too."

Seeing Paul's quizzical look, he added, "I could have told you about the car at church, but there was something else I wanted to say to you and Kate in private."

Kate's stomach tightened. *What now?*

Paul leaned against the counter. "Go ahead."

Jeff looked down at his plate and crumbled a bit of the last cookie between his fingers. "It's about Lisa. She had a really bad experience with a church when she was growing up."

"I'm sorry to hear that," Paul said. "Can you tell us what happened?"

Jeff paused for a long moment, then shook his head. "I don't want to gossip, so I think you'd better hear it from Lisa herself. I know she's been kind of prickly where you two are concerned"—he sent a quick glance Kate's way—"but maybe you could visit her sometime and get her to open up. I think she's been holding this stuff in way too long. She really is a great person," he said with a smile that reminded Kate once again of Andrew.

Paul nodded slowly. "I think you're right. We'll be praying about the best time for us to visit. God knows the best timing for all of this."

"Thanks a lot." Jeff's shoulders seemed to relax. "I didn't want to go into all of that at the meeting."

"You did the right thing," Paul said.

Jeff scooped up the last cookie from his plate. "Thanks again, Kate. The cookies were great."

Paul kissed her good-bye, then the two men hurried out the door.

Kate placed the rest of the cookies from the first batch on a decorated plate, deep in thought. So Lisa *had* been hurt by church people as a young girl. Kate picked up a cookie and chewed it slowly. She always said that baking helped her think things through. This time, it had given her something new to think about.

THE BELL OVER THE DOOR jingled when Kate entered Emma's Ice Cream Shop the next day. The smell of the mingled flavors of ice cream tingled her nose.

Kate smiled. That delicious scent always took her back to the ice-cream parlor she'd frequented in her childhood. She let out a contented sigh. Some things never changed.

Emma was nowhere to be seen, and Kate waited off to one side while Brenna served a noisy family of tourists.

When the group left the shop, Brenna turned toward her with a quizzical expression.

"You're turning into my best customer," Brenna said. "What would you like this time?"

"Two double cones, one mint chocolate chip, and the other one a combination triple fudge and chocolate ripple."

Surprise flickered in Brenna's eyes, and she gave Kate a questioning look.

Kate shrugged. "That is, if you think you have time to eat it before the next batch of tourists comes in."

A grin curved Brenna's lips. "I can get started on it anyway. I'll stick it in the freezer if I need to." She assembled the cones, then joined Kate at the same table they shared on Kate's previous visit.

Kate bit into the top scoop of mint chocolate chip. *Delicious.* "Did Micah happen to stop by yesterday?"

Brenna licked her cone and nodded. "Yeah, he came in

just before I went on my break." She did a double take and stared at Kate. "How did you know?"

"Oh, I talked with him yesterday afternoon. I got the impression he might be headed this way. We had quite a conversation," Kate continued, lowering her voice. "As a matter of fact, he told me that he was responsible for the vandalism that's been going on around town."

Brenna sucked in a breath and let it out slowly.

Kate eyed her closely. "But I'm not telling you anything you don't know, am I?"

Brenna opened her mouth, then closed it. Finally she shook her head. "No. I just didn't want to say anything. I know he's been in some trouble back in Nashville, but he's a nice guy, Mrs. Hanlon. Really, he is. And smart too."

Her eyes clouded. "But my mom would have freaked out if she thought I was getting involved with someone who was doing things like that. She already has problems with the idea that I'm old enough to be interested in boys."

Kate smiled, then took another lick of her ice cream. "I think that just goes along with being a mom. We all have a hard time accepting the fact that our babies are growing up."

Brenna eyed her doubtfully. "You really think she'll get over it?"

"I can't guarantee when that will happen, but most of us learn to deal with it eventually. Believe it or not, getting past your teens doesn't mean you've grown up. Becoming a mature adult is a lifelong process."

Brenna leaned back in her chair with a thoughtful look in her eyes. "I hope you're right that my mom will get used to the fact that I'm growing up. I'd really like for things to get back like they used to be, before she started worrying about me all the time."

Kate bit into her cone and chewed thoughtfully. Then she folded her arms on the table and leaned forward.

"There's something I still need to know, Brenna. What was it that you two threw off the bridge?"

Brenna took her time with another mouthful of ice cream, then she met Kate's eyes and nodded. "I guess it's okay to tell you now."

She looked around as if to make sure they were still alone. "Micah told me about his plan to help his aunt's dog win the show. Did he talk to you about that?"

Kate nodded.

"It was really stupid, if you ask me. Sweet, maybe, because he really wanted to help his aunt, but stupid. I mean, did he really think that upsetting the other dog owners would make any difference?" Brenna shook her head, looking like an adult bewildered by the childish actions of a little boy.

"He'd just bought a couple of cans of spray paint, and he brought them with him to the bridge. He was bragging about how he was going to put some graffiti on Mrs. Lambert's house after dark."

The air whooshed out of Kate's lungs. Spray paint on Renee's pristine house? She shuddered, thinking of what that would have done to Renee . . . and what Renee would have done to Micah if she'd ever learned he was the person responsible.

"Go on," she told Brenna.

"I kind of blew up at him." Brenna's eyes narrowed. "I told him it was a dumb thing to do, and he was only going to cause more problems for himself. We started arguing, and it got kind of loud, I guess. That was probably when you heard us."

"Then the white object I saw?"

"I finally convinced him not to do it. He promised me he'd get rid of the paint, but I told him I didn't know if I could trust him. So he threw the bag with the spray paint into the creek." A tiny grin tugged at her lips. "Then I yelled at him for littering."

Kate laughed along with her.

"I thought everything was okay after that, but then I heard about the toilet paper at the Wilsons' house and the sugar next to Mr. Philpott's truck. I knew it had to be Micah. I got really mad at him and told him I didn't want to talk to him anymore if he was going to keep on doing things like that."

A lightbulb turned on in Kate's head. That explained Micah's uncertainty about his reception at the ice-cream parlor the day before.

"I knew what was going on, but I didn't say anything." Brenna's cheeks turned a light shade of pink. "I didn't want to get him into trouble, but I didn't want to be involved with him either, if he was going to be doing that kind of stuff." She popped the last of her cone into her mouth and chewed it thoughtfully.

Kate reached across the table and squeezed Brenna's

hand. "For what it's worth, I believe you're right about Micah. I don't think he's a bad kid at all."

Brenna smiled, then Kate pushed back her chair and stood up. "I've got to get going, but I have one more request. If you wouldn't mind, Pastor Paul and I would like to come over and talk to your mother."

Brenna's eyes grew round, and Kate hastened to add, "Not about Micah. It's something else entirely. Do you think she might even be available tonight after supper?"

Brenna shook her head. "Probably not. They're taking inventory at Fancy Fabrics. Mom's boss told her she was going to have to work late tonight and all day tomorrow." Brenna wrinkled her nose. "She's going to be really cranky all weekend."

"Then how about Monday, after supper?"

"That's probably the best time. I'm glad you're going to talk to her, to be honest." Brenna's brown eyes danced with mischief. "But I'm glad I have to work on Monday evening so I won't be around when you do."

Chapter Seventeen

Mrs. Hanlon, we're ready for your report." Wilbur Dodson's paper-dry voice jolted Kate out of her thoughts.

She blinked at the trio of officers seated at the front table. Velma Hopkins regarded her with interest, but Lucy Mae never shifted her gaze from the tablet where she was scribbling notes.

One corner of Wilbur's mouth twitched repeatedly. Kate wondered if he'd had to speak to her more than once before she realized it.

"I'm sorry. What report do you mean?"

Finalizing preparations for the show was coming down to the wire, and the pressure seemed to be taking a toll on Wilbur's patience. The lines bracketing his narrow lips deepened.

"We're only two weeks away from the show, Mrs. Hanlon. Have you ordered the awards for those additional prizes you're so eager to hand out? This is why we've been meeting once a week. Things like that can't be left to the last minute. We have to be sure that none of the details slip through the cracks."

Kate straightened in her chair and spoke in a crisp tone. "I've ordered the awards as directed. I'm going to pick them up this coming week."

"That's fine, then."

Kate thought Wilbur looked almost disappointed at being deprived of something to fuss about.

"I want to bring up one last matter before we adjourn," Wilbur said. "As most of you know, Renee Lambert's Chihuahua is still missing. Personally, I don't know that we can hold out much hope for his recovery at this point. But I want to urge all our members to be on the lookout for anything that might lead to his safe return.

"It's disturbing to hear about this kind of thing happening to any loving dog owner, but especially when it's one of our own."

He curled his fingers into a fist, then smiled and reached for the gleaming new gavel that lay at his side. He picked it up and gave a sharp rap on the table. "That's all for today. Meeting adjourned."

Kate grabbed her handbag and stepped out of the meeting room, still deep in thought. How was she ever going to unravel this mystery? Maybe she needed to go back to the beginning and visit Copper Mill Park again.

Any evidence she might have missed before would surely be gone by now, but perhaps just by being in the same place . . .

"Kate?"

She turned and saw Lucy Mae hurrying toward her. "Could I talk to you for a minute?"

"Of course."

Lucy Mae led her into the space between two tall shelves of books and twisted her hands together. "Micah said he talked to you on Thursday after we saw you at the diner."

Kate nodded but didn't volunteer any information.

"I do wish he'd come to me first, but I'm glad he opened up to you." Lucy Mae heaved a deep sigh. "He told me that he was the one who dyed Maribeth's Pomeranian blue."

"I got the impression you suspected it even before he told you," Kate said gently.

"I'm afraid so. I found the label from a box of that temporary hair color when I was throwing some scraps in the trash the other night."

Lucy Mae blinked rapidly. "At first I was afraid he was going to start dyeing his hair in wild colors like his friends back in Nashville. But when Maribeth carried Mitzi into the beauty shop, and Betty mentioned the temporary dye, that's when I knew."

She looked at Kate, sadness filling her eyes. "You knew too, didn't you?"

"I was pretty sure. I'd heard a little about Micah's background, and when you hurried out of Betty's like that, I put two and two together. But I do think he's a nice boy at heart, and I'm glad he decided to own up to his actions."

Lucy Mae squared her shoulders. "He told me the rest of it too—about what he'd done at the Wilsons' and the Philpotts'. Then I made him tell Lawton."

Kate felt a twinge of sympathy for Micah. Three confessions in one day would have been a lot for anyone. "How did Lawton take it?"

Lucy Mae grimaced. "Let's just say they had a long talk. I really think Micah wants to turn his life around. He knows we've forgiven him, but he also understands we can't just let it go at that. He's agreed to apologize to the Wilsons, the Philpotts, and Maribeth and work out some sort of restitution. Maybe do some yard work for the Wilsons and wash and wax Lester's truck. As for Maribeth . . ." Her voice trailed off.

"There isn't anything he can do to help poor Mitzi at this point. With a dye job like that, I'm sure it won't wash out in time for the show. If she tries to bleach it, she'll ruin the condition of Mitzi's coat. I'm afraid she's just going to have to wait until a whole new coat grows back in before it's gone completely.

"Micah's talking about finding a part-time job so he can earn enough money to pay for Mitzi to make extra visits to the groomer until a new coat of fur replaces the old."

Kate nodded her approval. "All of that sounds good, and I'm glad he's willing to step up and take responsibility for what he's done. This could be a real turning point for him."

"That's what Lawton says." Lucy Mae pulled a tissue from her pocket and dabbed at her eyes. "This whole thing is really my fault, you know."

"Your fault? Micah said you hadn't put him up to anything."

"I'm not so sure." Lucy Mae sniffled, and two large tears rolled down her cheeks. This time she didn't bother to wipe them away. "Lawton's right; all I've talked about for weeks is the dog show and how much I want Sir Percival to win. Micah was trying to do something nice for me, even though the way he went about it was totally misguided."

Tears welled up again. "I wish I could take it all back. It's so easy to take things too seriously and let them get out of hand."

Kate gave Lucy Mae a quick hug. "I think we can all fall into that trap. But don't be too hard on yourself. This may turn out to be a blessing in disguise if it's the wake-up call Micah needed."

"Thanks, Kate. It's nice of you to say so."

Kate smiled as she patted Lucy Mae's arm, then turned to leave.

"Oh, wait," Lucy Mae said. "There's one more thing." She drew a deep breath. "Micah isn't the only one who needs to make amends. Do you remember those things I said about Renee and Kisses at Betty's a couple weeks ago?"

Kate nodded.

"I didn't plan to say any of that," Lucy Mae confided. "The words just popped out of my mouth, and it's been eating me alive ever since. Especially with little Kisses being stolen."

Her mouth twisted. "I know I need to do something about it, but I don't want to cause Renee any more pain than she's already going through."

Kate smiled and squeezed Lucy Mae's arm. "I think Renee would appreciate it if you told her the same thing you've told me. It'll do you both good. Why don't you stop by her house on your way home? She told me she was going to be making another round of phone calls this morning instead of coming to the meeting."

"Thanks, Kate. I'll do that." Lucy Mae plied her tissue once more, then her lips parted in a wobbly smile. "I'll collect my things from the meeting room and go see her right now."

Kate headed downstairs, rejoicing at the knowledge that a reconciliation was in the making.

Kate found Livvy in her office and lightly tapped on the door. Livvy looked up and smiled when she saw Kate.

"Hey, stranger. How are the plans for the dog show coming along?"

"Okay, I think. I just wish I knew more specifics about what I'm supposed to be doing. Making people welcome is one thing, but they tell me I'll have to help if problems arise. What problems? How am I supposed to help if I don't know what's going on myself?"

Livvy laughed. "Poor Kate. Is there anything I can do to help?"

"Honestly, I think I just needed a chance to blow off a little steam." Kate rolled her neck to loosen the tense muscles. "I guess it's the neat freak in me coming out, wanting everything to be in its place but not sure how to get it there. I'll just try to roll with the punches and hope everything comes out all right."

"I'm sure it will. And I hereby volunteer to come help out on show day with whatever it is you wind up doing." Livvy's face grew solemn. "By the way, have you seen Renee lately?"

"I stopped by her house yesterday afternoon." Kate's throat tightened at the memory. "She started to fill Kisses' water dish, then she caught herself and went across the room to water one of her plants instead. I don't think she realized that I noticed."

Kate leaned her elbows on Livvy's desk and cradled her chin in her hands. "Do you have any ideas? The only thing I can think of is to go back to the park and nose around again."

"Don't ask me. I'm the one who sent us off on that wild-goose chase for the designer tote, remember? Speaking of which, Ardith Bennett came in this morning. While I was checking out her books, she asked if we were still interested in buying the tote." Livvy chuckled. "I told her no."

Kate shook her head, weary with the frustration of it all. "I've followed several leads, but everything I've tracked down has led to a dead end."

Livvy leaned back in her chair and crossed her arms. "I saw a show once where an investigator said that the hardest crimes to solve are the random ones where there are no witnesses or obvious suspects, and the trail goes cold within hours."

Kate's shoulders slumped. "I'm afraid that's what we have here. I'm stumped."

Chapter Eighteen

W hat do you want?" Lisa Phillips peered out at Paul and Kate through the crack in her front door.

Kate's stomach tightened. She took a deep breath and said a quick prayer for a loving and grace-filled attitude toward Lisa as she and Paul tried to be peacemakers.

"We'd like to talk to you," Paul began. "Could we come in for a few minutes? We won't stay long."

Lisa wavered, as if she couldn't decide whether to open the door or slam it in their faces. Then she swung the door wide open, and she stepped back, allowing them to enter.

She waved them toward the couch and sat stiffly on the chair Brenna had occupied during Kate's previous visit.

Paul crossed his legs and laced his fingers around his knee. "We just wanted to stop by and try to clear the air a bit."

Kate saw Lisa's shoulders stiffen and her chin jut forward a fraction. This wasn't going to be easy.

She decided it was time for her to step in. "First of all, I need to apologize to you."

Lisa didn't show any signs of softening, but no angry words came spilling out of her mouth. Kate felt a flicker of hope.

She proceeded with caution. Bigger things were at stake than convincing Lisa that she was sorry for implicating Brenna in Kisses' disappearance. Lisa had been shouldering a load of pain all by herself for a long time. Lord willing, Kate and Paul could help ease her burden.

"We've enjoyed having Brenna in the youth group. She's a delightful girl and a real tribute to your ability as a mother."

Lisa's mouth relaxed, but her eyes remained wary. "But . . . ?"

Kate shook her head. "No but's. She's a wonderful girl, and that's the simple truth. The reason Skip and I wanted to talk with Brenna was to find out if she knew anything about something I saw fall into the creek during one of my walks. I never meant to accuse her of wrongdoing.

"And I'm sorry I didn't handle the situation as well as I could have when you arrived. You had every right to be upset when you found me here in your house talking to your daughter with a uniformed deputy. My actions caused you pain, and for that I'm truly sorry."

Lisa's chin began to tremble, and she pressed her lips tightly together. She bent forward and buried her face in her hands.

Kate longed to reach out and comfort her but held back, not knowing how Lisa would react to such an overture. She and Paul waited in silence until Lisa pulled herself together enough to raise her head and look at them through tear-soaked eyes.

"I can't believe you're saying that. You, the minister's wife, apologizing to me?"

"I'm the one who was in the wrong," Kate said simply.

Lisa swiped her cheek with her palm. "I don't know what to say. You're not the only one who needs to apologize, though. I was really awful to you at Abby Pippins' house. I was angry, but I didn't have any right to say those things in front of all those women. And then you left so I could stay. That just blew me away. I should have told you to come back inside right then. I'm so sorry."

"Apology accepted." Kate smiled.

Lisa closed her eyes and let out a long breath. "I haven't treated either one of you very well. This whole thing with Brenna reminded me of something I went through back when I was her age, and I guess it pushed a lot of the wrong buttons. I thought I was going to see the same thing happen all over again."

Both Kate and Paul kept still, waiting to see if Lisa would say anything more. Kate watched an inward struggle play out on the other woman's face.

Finally Lisa spoke. "Brenna doesn't even know everything that happened. I couldn't bring myself to tell her. I see so much of me in her, and maybe that's what scares me the most. Believe it or not, I was a regular in the youth group at the church my parents went to when I was growing up."

Kate wasn't able to smother a gasp of surprise.

"Yeah, I guess that does come as a shock, doesn't it?" Lisa's smile faded. "My parents thought it was great that I spent most of my time with other kids from church. I guess they figured that would keep me on the straight and narrow."

Lisa shifted in her chair and stared at a point on the wall above Kate's head. "Then I told them I was pregnant, and their Christian love went right out the window."

Tears stung Kate's eyes. "I'm so sorry."

Lisa drew a ragged breath. "The whole church turned against me too. My parents didn't kick me out of the house, but they treated me like they were ashamed that I was part of their family. They went to church every time the doors were open, the same as usual, but I couldn't go back. I wasn't welcome there anymore."

Her voice wavered. "Even the other kids in the youth group turned their backs on me. It was like I was all alone in the world."

Suddenly Lisa's face softened. "Then Brenna was born, and suddenly there was someone who belonged to me again. She's all I have."

"Did things ever get better between you and your parents?" Paul asked.

Lisa shook her head. "They kept on living their perfect

lives and made sure I knew I wasn't welcome any longer. I stayed with them until I graduated from high school, but I haven't seen them since I left home."

"Oh my." Kate pressed her fingers to her lips.

The sadness in Lisa's eyes was unmistakable. "They made it clear they'd be much happier if I weren't around."

Paul uncrossed his legs and leaned forward. "It makes a lot more sense to me now why you haven't wanted to come to church with Brenna."

"It's not just your church," Lisa corrected. "It's any church. I'd already seen an example of so-called love in action. I didn't want to put myself through that again."

A sob shook her, and she gripped the arms of the chair. "There's one thing I've always wanted to know. Where was that forgiveness they always talked about?"

This time Kate did go over and wrap her arms around the other woman. Lisa leaned against her for a moment, accepting the comfort she offered. Kate felt as though her heart would break at the thought of how much pain this young woman had endured.

"I'm so sorry," she whispered again. "With your background, I'm surprised you even let Brenna walk through the doors of Faith Briar."

Lisa shrugged and mopped at her face. "A neighbor started taking her to Sunday school when she was little. She seemed to like it, so I let her go. I didn't think it would do her any harm."

Her face clouded. "But she's getting older now and

starting to look at boys. I worry about her when she's there. I worry about her anywhere, for that matter. I don't want her to make the same mistake I made."

Kate gave her a final squeeze and returned to the couch. "That's hard, I know. It isn't easy for any of us moms."

Lisa looked from Paul to Kate. "Thank you both. I know it couldn't have been easy for you to come over and talk to me like this after the things I've said."

"We had to," Paul said, then he smiled. "We wanted to. We didn't want to have the rift between us continue. And we wanted to let you know that we care about you and that God loves you very much."

He stood and held out his hand to help Kate to her feet. Each of them gave Lisa a quick hug, then together they started toward the door.

"I can understand your reluctance to have anything to do with church after what you've been through," Paul said, "but we'll be praying that God will heal the hurts of the past and that you'll begin to experience a true reflection of his love through his people."

Lisa nodded slowly. "I think I'm beginning to see that not all church people are like my parents. Not if you two and Jeff are any example." A light blush stained her cheeks as soon as she spoke the words.

Kate was reminded of the way Brenna looked every time Micah's name was mentioned. She reached out and gave Lisa's arm a quick squeeze. "Call us if you need us. We want you to know that we're here for you."

Kate's cell phone buzzed, and she opened her handbag to dig it out. "I'm sorry. I meant to turn this off before we came."

She stepped out onto the porch to take the call while Paul said his good-byes to Lisa.

"Missus Hanlon?" Skip's voice crackled with excitement on the other end. "You have to come down to the office right now. You'll never believe what's happening."

Chapter Nineteen

Skip didn't give you any idea what's going on?"

"No." Kate swayed on the seat of Paul's pickup as he rounded the corner onto Euclid Road and headed for the deputy's office at the Town Hall. "All he would say was that we needed to get down there right away."

"Do you think something's wrong?"

"I don't think so. At least I hope not. He sounded excited, but in a good way."

Paul pulled into a parking spot and circled around the front of the truck to help Kate step down to the sidewalk.

Together they hurried up the walkway of the Town Hall and climbed the concrete stairs that led to the entrance. Once inside the building, they headed straight for the deputy's office, where they found Skip and two people Kate didn't recognize huddled around a desk at the far side of the room.

"Hi, Skip," she said. "What's going on?"

Skip turned, a wide grin splitting his freckled face. "Thanks for coming down. I wanted you to see this. You guys must have been doing a lot of praying. I think we're looking at a miracle here."

He said something to the other couple, who stepped aside to reveal what they'd been huddled around.

Kate gasped, then ran across to the desk, where a little Chihuahua with enormous brown eyes and floppy ears sat. He looked up at Kate with a plaintive expression, and the tip of his tail quivered.

"It can't be." She reached down to pull the tiny dog into her arms. "Kisses! I can't believe it's you."

She cuddled him close, and he shivered in her arms. Kate stroked her hand along his back and frowned when she felt his ribs under her fingertips. He must have lost weight during his time away from home. No matter. Renee would have him back to his pampered self in no time. She smiled at the thought of Renee concocting special tidbits for Kisses in her kitchen.

"Where did you find him?" Paul asked Skip.

"Not me. It was those flyers Miz Lambert put up. They actually worked." Skip pointed to the other couple. "These folks found him. This is Mr. and Mrs. Murphy from Pine Ridge."

Kate looked at the tall, rawboned man and the ill-groomed blonde woman, and her memory stirred. She had seen them once before when she visited the Country Diner with Paul, shortly after Kisses vanished.

Mrs. Murphy stepped forward and extended her hand to Kate. "We found him runnin' around the SuperMart parkin' lot. He looked lost and lonely, and I couldn't bear to think of him out there loose with all those cars and trucks around."

She scratched the little dog under the chin and cooed at him. "He's such a sweet little guy. He came right to me when I called to him. I was all ready to take him in and give him a good home, but Clifford here"—she nodded to indicate her husband—"remembered seeing a flyer with a picture that looked just like him."

"That's right," he said with a broad smile. "I know how much Cissy would have loved to keep him, but it would have been wrong to take him away from his rightful owner."

Kisses wriggled in Kate's arms, and she set him back down on the desk.

"I know how attached I felt after just a few minutes with him," Cissy added. "I can only imagine how heartbroken his real owner must be."

Paul exchanged glances with Kate. "You have no idea," he said.

Clifford picked up the story. "We drove over to where I remembered seeing one of the flyers. I wrote down the phone numbers and called the sheriff's office in Pine Ridge. They told me to bring the dog down here to Deputy Spencer, and here we are."

Kate looked at Skip. "Aren't you going to call Renee?"

He shook his head. "I'm going to take him over to her place myself. Knowing how excited she'll be, I didn't think she needed to be out driving."

"Good point," Paul agreed.

"Do you mind if we come along?" Kate asked.

"Sure. You folks should come too," he said to the Murphys. "I know Miz Lambert's going to want to thank you yourself."

"I CAN'T BELIEVE it's over," Kate told Paul as they followed Skip's SUV down Main Street, with Kisses perched on the front passenger seat of the deputy's vehicle. The Murphys brought up the rear of the procession in their rusty Toyota.

"I wonder if Skip should have called Renee and broken the news to her first," Paul said. "I hope it isn't too much of a shock for her to have Kisses appear at her door like that."

"No, I think Skip was right. She would have jumped in her car and driven straight to his office. Given the state she's been in lately, I don't think she would have been safe out on the roads, even if she does live only a couple of blocks away."

They turned left on Smith Street, then right on Ashland, coming to a stop in front of Renee's house on the corner. Kate tried to picture the happy reunion in her mind. Renee was going to be shocked, no doubt about it. But she would be thrilled, oh so thrilled, to have her little Kisses home again after all this time.

A dash of disappointment mingled with Kate's excitement. While she was overjoyed at the thought of Kisses and Renee being reunited, there was still the knowledge that she hadn't played an active part in bringing that about.

But she had prayed, and that thought warmed her. She was wrong to think she had no part in bringing about Kisses' return. Prayer was the very best thing anyone could have done.

After the little caravan had stopped in front of Renee's house, Skip gathered Kisses in his arms, looking as excited as Kate felt.

"Why don't you and Paul go on up and ring the door-bell?" he said. "I'll wait off to one side, and you can pre-pare her for the big surprise."

And catch her if she faints, Kate thought as Paul rang the doorbell.

Renee greeted them wearing a pink cotton duster. From her rumpled appearance, Kate wondered if she had even bothered to get dressed that day.

"Hi, Renee. We brought someone to see you."

"This isn't a good time. Mother's already in bed." Renee's gaze shifted to the couple standing directly behind the Hanlons. She pulled the housedress tighter around her neck and leveled an admonishing look at Kate. "I'm really not prepared for company, Kate."

"Oh, I think you'll welcome this." Kate smiled and beckoned to Skip, who stepped into Renee's view.

Renee stared wordlessly at the dog in Skip's arms. Then her hand flew to her mouth. "Oh my. Can it be?"

She stepped out onto the porch and held out her arms. "My baby is home again. Come to Mommy, my Little Umpkins!"

Renee held the tiny dog against her chest and rocked

back and forth. "You're home. You're home," she crooned. "Oh, Mommy missed you so!"

Tears streamed down her cheeks, but Renee didn't seem to care. Her voice wobbled when she turned to Skip. "Thank you so much."

"It wasn't me, Miz Lambert." Skip grinned from ear to ear. "It was these folks, the Murphys."

Kisses wriggled in Renee's arms, and she rubbed the spot between his ears with her forefinger. "Let's get you inside, Umpkins. Come on in, all of you. I can't thank you properly out here."

They trooped into the house. Paul put his arm around Kate's shoulder, and she leaned against him, blinking back tears. It looked like Renee was going to get her happy ending after all.

"However did you find him?" Holding Kisses in one arm, Renee pulled a tissue from the box on the little table with her free hand and blotted her damp cheeks.

The Murphys recounted their story of spotting Kisses in the SuperMart parking lot and Clifford remembering the flyers.

"There, you see?" Renee gave Kate a watery smile. "I knew it was worth our time putting up those flyers. They helped bring my baby home."

Kisses squirmed again, and she set him down near his bed. He walked over and sniffed at the cushion, then backed away and shivered nervously on the carpet.

Kate frowned. What was wrong? She'd expected Kisses to go wild with delight the moment he returned home. Instead, he sat trembling on the floor, staring up at the group as if wondering what was going to happen next.

Something didn't seem right. Thinking back to the scene in Skip's office, Kate remembered that Kisses had seemed only mildly pleased when she and Paul arrived. She hadn't thought it terribly odd at the time, considering all the upheaval he'd been through. But surely seeing Renee again should have sent him into a frenzy of excitement.

Renee noticed it too. She squatted down in front of Kisses and gave him an appraising look. "Are you not feeling well?" she cooed. "Was it horrible for momma's precious baby to live outdoors like a wild animal?"

Tears spilled from her eyes again, and she looked up at Kate. "I think he's angry with me for leaving him alone that day."

She turned back to Kisses, and her voice cracked. "Oh, my sweet Umpkins, can you ever forgive me?"

Kate laid her hand on Renee's shoulder. "He's been through a lot. I'm sure it will take some time for him to readjust."

Renee sniffed, and Kate helped her get to her feet.

"You're probably right. What I want to do is just scoop him up and hold him tight, but I guess I'll have to let him get reacclimated at his own pace."

She swiped at her cheeks with her fingers, then walked over to where the Murphys stood and took each one by the hand.

"I've been trying to keep up my courage, but I'll admit I was very near to losing hope of ever seeing my precious baby again. I cannot thank you enough for bringing him home to me. I don't know how I can ever repay you."

The Murphys exchanged glances, then Clifford lowered his head and cleared his throat. "Well, ma'am . . ."

Cissy Murphy looked at Renee and smiled expectantly.

"Oh!" Renee seemed taken aback. "Oh, of course, the reward!"

Clifford shuffled his feet. "Well, I hated to bring it up, but—"

"Whatever you think is fair." Cissy put in.

"Just a moment." Renee touched her finger to her lips and blew a kiss at the little dog. "Don't worry, Umpkins. Mommy's going to be right back."

She left the room and returned with her checkbook and a pen. "What were your names again?"

"Clifford and Cissy Murphy." Clifford spelled it for her.

Renee filled out the check and signed it with a flourish, then tore it from the checkbook and handed it to the waiting couple.

When Clifford looked at the check, his eyes flared wide. Cissy peered over his shoulder, and Kate heard her gasp.

"Why, ma'am," Clifford began, not bothering to hide his wide grin. "We never expected—"

Cissy grabbed his arm. "He means to say you're a very kind woman, and we thank you for your generosity."

"That's right." Clifford's head bobbed up and down. "Well, we'll leave you two to your happy reunion."

"Thank you again," Renee said, "from the bottom of my heart."

"Glad to have been of service." Clifford nodded again, and the two scuttled out the front door.

Kate looked back at Renee, unable to shake a sense of foreboding. "You must have been pretty generous, Renee. May I ask how much you gave them?"

"One thousand dollars." Renee capped her pen and set it on the table beside the checkbook.

"A thousand!" Skip jerked to attention. "If you'll pardon me for saying so, Miz Lambert, that's an awful lot of money."

"And I would have gladly given more. I can't place a monetary value on having my family whole again. Getting my Little Umpkins back is simply priceless."

She looked down at Kisses, who had curled up on the floor next to his cushion. Her forehead puckered. "Whatever can be wrong with him? Normally, he loves his little bed. He isn't acting like himself at all."

Renee bent to lift the little Chihuahua and carried him to the couch, where she set him on her lap and began running her fingers along his thin little body.

"I should call the vet to come over and give him a thorough examination. He may have an injury I haven't noticed. Or even worms, after eating heaven knows what out in the wild." She shuddered. "Here, Umpkins, turn over on your back and let Mommy . . . *Ahhh!*" A horrified gasp burst from her lips.

Kate's heart stopped. "Renee, what is it? What's wrong?"

"Look!" Renee pointed to the inner part of the dog's right hind leg. "Do you see that patch of white hair? Kisses doesn't have anything like that."

She stood up and held the Chihuahua at arm's length. "I've been duped. This is an impostor!"

Skip was out the front door in a flash. Kate followed on his heels.

Clifford Murphy had started the Toyota and was about to pull away from the curb when Skip sprinted into the street and held up his hand in a commanding gesture.

Clifford braked and rolled down his window. "What's the trouble, Deputy?"

"Please turn the car off and step outside, Mr. Murphy. I need to talk to you for a minute."

Clifford hesitated, then switched off the key and climbed out. Cissy stepped out the passenger side. "Is there some kind of problem?"

"The problem is, the dog you brought back is not Miz Lambert's Chihuahua."

"What are you talking about?" Cissy bustled around the rear of the car and stood beside her husband. "How could she possibly say that? That dog is a dead ringer for the one on the flyer."

Skip gave her a long measuring look and planted his hands on his hips. "I've known Miz Lambert since I was knee high. You can take it from me, she knows every inch of that dog, and this one isn't hers." He held out his hand, palm up.

Clifford stared at Skip's hand for a moment, then he

reached inside his shirt pocket, drew out the check, and laid it in Skip's hand.

"Come on, Cissy. We might as well go home."

His wife sniffed. "This is what you get for trying to do a good deed." With a last longing glance at the check, she flounced around the Toyota and got back inside.

"At least Miz Lambert didn't wind up paying a thousand dollars for a dog that doesn't belong to her," Skip said to Kate as they walked back to the house. "That was a close call."

"Yes, but we still aren't any closer to bringing the real Kisses home, and now Renee's emotions are even more fragile. I wish I would have noticed . . ." She let her words trail off.

Back inside the house, they found Renee huddled on the sofa, just as Kate had seen her the day Kisses disappeared. Paul stood beside her holding the box of tissues. He looked at Kate with a helpless expression.

Kate slid onto the couch and cradled Renee in her arms as she would a brokenhearted child. Kate was shocked when she felt Renee's shoulder blades standing out sharply through the thin cotton fabric of her duster. "I'm so sorry, Renee."

"I can't believe I was taken in by that pretender." Renee looked at the false Kisses in disgust. "How could I ever have mistaken him for my precious Umpkins?"

Renee gasped and clapped her hands to her mouth. "Oh, I hope Kisses never finds out about this."

Kate noticed that the older woman's hands were trembling. "Renee, have you had anything to eat today?"

"Oh, I'm fine. I had some crackers and milk earlier."

"That isn't very substantial. Why don't I fix you a nice cup of Earl Grey tea just the way you like it, and maybe a little soup or a sandwich?"

When she got up and started for the kitchen, Skip stepped forward. "I'm real sorry, Miz Lambert. I sure didn't think it would turn out like this."

He looked down at the small dog on the floor and scratched his head. "What do you want me to do with this little guy? I could turn him in to the Humane Society. Or do you want to keep him, just in case . . ."

Renee's eyes flashed. "Absolutely not! I would never betray Kisses like that. I have to believe that somehow he'll find his way home again."

Her face crumpled, and she wailed aloud. "Oh, my Little Umpkins. Where are you?"

Kate looked at Paul from the kitchen doorway and knew the same thought was running through both their minds: it was going to be a long night.

Chapter Twenty

I thought Renee was going to blow a gasket when Skip suggested that she might want to keep the other dog," Kate said to Livvy and LuAnne the following afternoon at the Country Diner. "The look she gave him should have turned him to stone on the spot."

LuAnne shook her head. "I've seen that look before. Poor Skip. I'll bet he skedaddled right after that."

"He didn't stay long." Kate admitted with a chuckle.

"That other Chihuahua must have looked a lot like Kisses to fool Renee for even a moment," Livvy said.

"It was amazing," Kate said. "He really was a dead ringer for Kisses, except for that patch of white hair."

"Poor little thing." Livvy pursed her lips. "What's going to happen to him?"

"He already has a new home." Kate smiled at the surprised look on her friends' faces. "I just happened to know that Brenna Phillips has been wanting a small dog. Now she has one."

"Isn't that perfect?" LuAnne beamed. "What about Renee's mama? How did she take all the goin's-on?"

Kate laughed. "Would you believe she slept through the whole thing? And it's probably just as well."

"I'm sure you had your hands full enough just dealing with Renee," Livvy said.

Kate nodded. "We didn't leave until nearly midnight. I fixed Renee some chicken noodle soup. She said she didn't have any appetite, so I sat with her until she finished most of it."

She drummed her fingers on the table. "When I hugged her, I could tell she's lost weight. I don't think she's been eating right since all this began."

"It wouldn't surprise me," Livvy said. "She's been going through a grieving process right now, just as if she'd lost a person she loves."

"That's exactly what's happened." Kate looked at her two friends. "I'm really worried about her. When she found out that little dog wasn't Kisses, she was so distraught, I thought she'd disintegrate right there before our eyes. We just *have* to find Kisses. Why don't we do a little brainstorming?"

"Sounds good to me." Livvy pulled a notebook and pen from her handbag. "I can take notes while you go back over everything point by point."

"That's a good idea." LuAnne nodded her approval. "When a bloodhound loses a trail, he has to go back to the last place he had a scent and try to pick it up again. So where's our last scent?" She and Livvy eyed Kate expectantly.

"That's the problem. There really isn't any." Kate ticked off the points as Livvy jotted them down in her notebook.

"After seeing Renee in action at the dog-club meeting, I thought at first that one of the members might be involved.

"I also considered the possibility of a dognapping ring, but I can't find any evidence to substantiate it. I can't disprove it either, so we probably shouldn't cross it off the list just yet, even though there haven't been any other dognappings in the area."

"What about whoever's behind all the vandalism that's been goin' on around town?" LuAnne asked, a grim expression on her face. "Every one of those victims owns a dog."

"That's right," Livvy exclaimed, her eyes wide. "Maybe that's the missing connection!"

Kate hated to burst her friend's bubble. She shook her head. "You two are thinking exactly like I did until, well, let's just say I have it on good authority that the vandalism has been nipped in the bud. So that isn't a factor anymore."

"Do you know who was involved?" Livvy asked.

Kate chose her words carefully. "I think it's best if I just say that the mayor has the situation under control."

LuAnne quirked an eyebrow. "Well, that's good to know. About it being over, I mean. Lawton Briddle has been tellin' everybody he was goin' to put a stop to it, and I guess he did."

Livvy poised her pen over her notebook. "Okay, what else do we have?"

Kate shrugged. "Renee thought at first she'd receive a ransom demand, but nobody has called asking for money."

Except for the Murphys, she thought. The couple had seemed awfully eager to leave as soon as Renee's unexpectedly large check was in their hands.

"Earth to Kate." Livvy snapped her fingers.

Kate blinked. "Sorry. I was just woolgathering."

"Must have been an awfully interesting sheep," LuAnne teased.

Livvy leaned forward, her eyes sparkling. "I know that look. What's up, Sherlock?"

"Do either of you know a couple named Clifford and Cissy—"

"Murphy," LuAnne cut in. "The ones from Pine Ridge? Yeah, they come in here every so often when Loretta's meat loaf is on special. Why? What have they done now?"

Something in LuAnne's tone made Kate feel like she might finally be on the right track.

"They're the ones who turned in the phony Kisses last night," Kate continued.

"Oh, brother." LuAnne leaned back in the booth and rolled her eyes. "They're a pair, those two. Always tryin' some get-rich-quick scheme.

"First, it was worm farming, then they were gonna make big money raisin' garlic. Last I heard, they had some notion they could make a fortune gettin' other people to sign up for some kind of pyramid sales thing."

She shook her head. "They'll try almost anything to make a fast buck."

Kate quivered like a bird dog on the scent. "Including trying to palm off a dog they knew wasn't the right one in order to get a reward?"

"I wouldn't put it past 'em," LuAnne said flatly.

Livvy drew in her breath. "Do you think that's what they tried to do last night?"

"I don't know," Kate said. "But I'm going to find out."

"ARE WE GETTING CLOSE?" Kate steered her Honda around a bend in the two-lane highway that led from Copper Mill to Pine Ridge.

"I think so." LuAnne peered at the map printout she was holding. "It looks like we have a half mile or so to go before we turn off. Wouldn't you figure they'd live out on some back road?"

Kate waited until a furniture van passed by, then she checked for oncoming traffic before she risked a glance at the map herself.

"I think you're right. It shouldn't be much farther now."

Kate directed her eyes back onto the road. "I'm glad you were able to come with me."

"No problem. Things tend to be pretty slow during this time of the afternoon. J.B. and Loretta can handle anything that comes up until I get back."

After their brainstorming session at the diner, the three friends had hurried over to the library, where Livvy pulled out a Pine Ridge phone directory to look up the Murphys' street address.

Armed with the information, Kate had used one of the library's computers to pinpoint the location on the Internet and print out a map with driving directions to their home.

Livvy had used up her afternoon break time, so when Kate announced her intention of confronting the shady couple alone, LuAnne had insisted on going along, telling Livvy she would play Watson to Kate's Sherlock just this once.

"I'm not about to let you go up there by yourself," she had said in a tone that brooked no argument. "Not with a couple like the Murphys."

Kate was grateful for friends like Livvy and LuAnne, who were always willing to back her up.

"See that?" LuAnne pointed to a small road intersecting the highway. "I think it's the turnoff right up there."

Kate slowed and put her blinker on, then made a right turn. The narrow road wound its way back through thick stands of hickories, hemlocks, and ash trees that arched over the roadway. Kate found the effect almost oppressive.

If someone wanted to cover up an activity like a dog theft, a location like this—away from neighbors and the likelihood of being stumbled upon by accident—would make an ideal spot. Suddenly, she was doubly glad for her friend's presence.

She pulled well off the edge of the road and turned to LuAnne. "Before we go in, I want you to know what's in the back of my mind. I have no idea what we're going to find out here. It may turn out to be nothing more than a wild-goose chase.

"Even if it turns out that the Murphys knowingly brought in a counterfeit Kisses so they could claim the reward, they didn't get away with the money. After all, Skip retrieved the check, so they can argue that no actual harm has been done."

LuAnne pressed her lips together in a grim line. "Except to Renee."

Kate tapped her thumbs on the steering wheel. "It's just that something you said back at the diner keeps gnawing at me. You told Livvy and me that these people are always looking for ways to get easy money and aren't too particular about how they go about it."

LuAnne grunted. "That's a polite way to put it."

Kate spoke slowly, struggling to voice the thought that had been forming in her mind ever since their earlier discussion.

"What if they took Kisses and sold him immediately, then saw the flyers and jumped at the chance to make a little more cash?"

"Kind of like double-dipping, you mean? Get money once for poor little Kisses and then again when they turned in his look-alike for the reward?" LuAnne thought a moment, then nodded. "That's the kind of thing that would make sense to them."

"It would appeal to anyone with a greedy, grasping nature," Kate added. "In fact, the reward Renee gave them might even have amounted to more than what they sold Kisses for."

"You just may be onto something." LuAnne's eyes lit up. "Let's go check it out."

Kate put the car in motion again. She drove around a couple of curves that set her teeth on edge, then she spotted a small-frame house set back in a clearing off the road.

"This must be it," LuAnne said.

Kate turned into the driveway, her tires crunching on the gravel. As a precaution, she turned the car around before she parked so it was pointing back toward the road. In the event they had to make a hasty getaway, she wanted to give herself every possible advantage.

Clifford Murphy stepped outside before they reached the porch. "Afternoon, what can I do for . . ."

His voice trailed off, and his jaw sagged when he recognized Kate.

"Hello, Mr. Murphy," Kate said. "We've come to talk to you."

"Who is it, hon?" Cissy pushed past her husband and froze when she saw Kate. "What are you doin' here?"

"Just a friendly visit," LuAnne said. She regarded the house, from its untidy porch to the lace curtains that hung at a slightly crooked angle in the front window. "Cozy little place you've got here."

Cissy drew back and stared at LuAnne suspiciously. "We like it."

While they were talking, Kate studied the property, looking for any signs of canine life.

No kennels, no doggie toys, no yapping. Not even any telltale deposits on the lawn.

Kate wondered whether she was barking up the wrong tree, but the memory of Renee's tear-ravaged face spurred her to press on. She took a step closer to the porch.

"We'd like to ask you a few questions, if you don't mind."

Cissy and Clifford shifted uncomfortably where they stood and exchanged glances.

"That depends," Clifford said slowly. "What kind of questions?"

Kate's pulse quickened. This was her opportunity. "Where did the dog you turned in last night actually come from?"

She held her breath. She knew it was a long shot. She had no proof that the Murphys hadn't found the little Chihuahua exactly as they said, scampering around the SuperMart parking lot. If they stuck to their story, she would have no way to pursue the matter further.

The Murphys stood stock-still for a moment. Then Clifford's shoulders slumped, and he looked at his wife. "I knew we weren't going to be able to pull that one off."

Cissy smacked his shoulder. "You just hush. They can't prove anything."

She turned to Kate. "We didn't get to keep that check, so we haven't done anything wrong, not technically, anyway."

LuAnne rolled her eyes and gave Kate an "I told you so" look.

Kate held up her hands. "We're not trying to stir up trouble." *Unless it turns out you stole Kisses and ripped Renee's heart out in the process*, she thought. "We just want to know more about where that dog came from."

The Murphys looked at each other for a long moment.

"Might as well tell 'em," Clifford said. "I've got a feeling we're not gonna get any peace until we do."

Cissy threw her hands up in the air. "All right, have it your way."

She stepped to the edge of the porch and looked down at Kate. "We'd seen the flyers around town. Who could miss 'em? They're everywhere! But we didn't think anything about it at the time.

"We were over at a swap meet in Chattanooga this past weekend, and one of the vendors was selling a little dog real cheap. The minute we laid eyes on it, we knew it looked just like the one on that flyer, and—"

LuAnne folded her arms. "And so you figured you'd just make yourselves some easy cash."

Cissy's shoulders stiffened. "Well, who was to say it wasn't really that poor dog on the flyer? He's a dead ringer for the one who's missing. We just wanted to reunite him with his rightful owner."

Kate, LuAnne, and even Clifford stared at her in stunned silence.

Cissy shrugged. "Well, you never know."

Clifford moved up to stand beside his wife. "They wanted twenty dollars for him, and we happened to remember that the owner was offering a reward for the lost dog.

"We figured if there was a reward, it had to be more than twenty dollars. We'd at least break even, and maybe make a nice little profit if things went well. It seemed like a good business investment."

Cissy picked up the thread of the story. "So we bought him and brought him home with us. Clifford spent some time in Copper Mill on Monday, asking around just to make sure the real dog hadn't been turned in already.

When he found out he hadn't, Clifford came back home, and we called the sheriff. And you know the rest."

"We never expected a reward like that." Clifford looked down at the porch steps and shook his head. "I thought my teeth would drop out when I saw the size of that check. Nine hundred and eighty dollars of pure profit. You don't come across a deal like that every day." When he finally looked up, his face was a picture of utter dejection.

Kate studied the couple. The story sounded logical, at least to their way of thinking. She felt inclined to believe that was the way it happened.

Still, it didn't answer her other question.

She said casually, "LuAnne thought you might have been in Copper Mill the Saturday he went missing. It sure is a shame you didn't find him then."

Clifford rubbed the back of his neck. "Man, I wish we had! That way we'd have been able to keep that check, and we'd be in clover right now."

He gave a long, low whistle. "Imagine, givin' somebody a thousand dollars for a dog that's only worth twenty."

Kate nodded. That settled things in her mind. It was evident the Murphys had no idea of the actual market value of a pedigreed Chihuahua.

"I guess that's all we need to know." She turned back toward the car, and LuAnne followed suit.

"Wait a minute!" Cissy's shrill voice rang out from the porch. "What about our dog?"

"Your dog?" LuAnne's face was a study in bewilderment.

Cissy set her hands on her hips. "Yeah! We paid

twenty dollars for that mutt. That makes him our property, and we want him back."

Kate reached into the car and pulled out her handbag. She drew two ten-dollar bills from her wallet and walked over to place them in Cissy Murphy's hand.

"How about if I just reimburse you for the dog and save you all the added expense of food and supplies and vet fees?"

Cissy rubbed the bills together between her thumb and forefinger. Finally, she nodded.

"Yeah, I guess that'll work." She held the money up to Clifford. "Well, we didn't make the big bucks, but at least we broke even."

"DID YOU EVER SEE the likes of those two?" LuAnne said on their way back to the highway. "I feel like I need to take a shower."

"I know what you mean," Kate said as she guided the Honda onto the highway. "So, what do you think Sherlock and Watson would do next?"

LuAnne gave one of her rich, hearty laughs and propped her elbow on the window ledge. "My grandpa would've said it was time to load 'em back in the truck and call it a day. But we can't do that."

"No," Kate said, "not yet. So . . ."

LuAnne grinned. "You got it, darlin'. These bloodhounds are gonna keep right on sniffin'."

Chapter Twenty-One

After lunch the following Monday, Kate drove to the Mercantile for some supplies. After returning to her car, she placed the shopping bag on the front seat and reached inside to pull out the items she'd just purchased.

She had spent the previous evening trying out more no-bake cookie recipes, and that morning she had piled a variety of the tasty treats on a decorative plastic plate to take to Crystal Newcomb. From what she had heard from Paul about Daniel's wife, Crystal sounded like someone in dire need of companionship—just the kind of person the Friendship Club was trying to reach out to.

The cookies would be her gift to Crystal, but she wanted to get a couple of things for the Newcomb children as well. She had guessed at their ages. Paul had indicated they were both preschoolers but hadn't specified how old they were.

Kate peeled the price stickers off two coloring books, a box of crayons, and a pair of small stuffed animals. Preschoolers loved bright colors, and the soft toys would be suitable for either a boy or a girl.

Now to put Phase Two of her plan for the day in motion.

She had timed her visit for early afternoon, hoping that once she and Crystal had a chance to get acquainted, the younger woman might be open to accompanying her to the Friendship Club meeting.

To make sure mothers could attend the weekly meetings, Phoebe West had secured the services of a high-school girl to babysit the children in Abby's backyard while their mothers relaxed and enjoyed getting to know the other women.

Kate tried to imagine the loneliness of someone who was virtually isolated, with two small children and little interaction with other adults. Paul said the Newcombs didn't even have a phone.

Kate turned her key in the ignition and started the engine, then she reached into her handbag for the address she'd written on a piece of paper. She burrowed deeper, rummaging through the items that filled the space.

Where did that paper go?

Muttering under her breath, Kate removed the contents one item at a time: lipstick, cell phone, wallet, a pen, a small hairbrush and mirror.

She turned the handbag upside down and shook it, but no paper fluttered out.

Now what? Kate returned the items to the handbag—all but the cell phone. She would call Paul and get the address from him again.

When she punched in his number, she heard a loud beep. Surprised, Kate looked down at the phone in her hand and saw that the display read "low battery."

Rats. She had meant to put it on the charger the night before, but she'd been so immersed in her baking, she'd forgotten. *The one time I forget to charge my phone* . . . She tossed the phone back into her handbag.

She knew the Newcombs lived somewhere west of town, but that wasn't enough to get her there. She would have to stop by Paul's office and get the address from him. Thankfully, it wouldn't be too far out of her way.

"WHAT DO YOU THINK?" Daniel Newcomb wiped the sweat from his forehead with a bandanna and leaned against the lawn-mower handle while Paul inspected his handiwork.

"Nice job. I don't know when I've seen the church lawn look better." Paul couldn't help but notice the pride that lit Daniel's eyes.

Thanks, Lord. He wondered how long it had been since the man had heard a bit of genuine praise.

"After you put the mower back in the shed, why don't you meet me in my office? Millie put a gallon of iced tea in the fridge. I'll get us a couple of glasses."

Daniel grinned. "Sounds good to me."

A few minutes later, he sat in the visitor's chair near Paul's desk and accepted a large tumbler of tea. Ice cubes clinked against the glass when he took a long, deep drink.

"How's the job hunt going?" Paul asked.

Daniel shook his head, and his eyes dimmed a bit. He glanced around as if looking for a coaster, then set the glass on Paul's desk blotter.

"Nothing yet. Frankly, if it wasn't for you and the odd

jobs you've been givin' me, we'd be eatin' beans every night."

Paul frowned and tapped his fingertips together. "Have you given any thought to what I suggested about finding a job that's geared to your talents?"

Daniel took another gulp of tea, then leaned forward, holding the glass in both hands.

"Yeah, I have. I spent some time the other day tryin' to figure out what I enjoy and what I'm good at, like you said. I enjoy bein' outdoors and workin' with my hands."

He rolled his shoulders. "Bein' cooped up in a factory or warehouse all day long puts me on edge to begin with. I never can seem to relax. Maybe that's part of the reason I'm always messin' up."

"You may have a point." Paul leaned back and crossed his ankle over his knee. "Anytime you try to do something completely at odds with the unique way you're created, that starts you off at a disadvantage."

He thought for a moment. "So you'd prefer some kind of outdoor, manual work?"

Daniel's eyes lit up again. "Yeah. Kind of like what I've been doin' here around the church. I enjoy it so much, it doesn't even seem like work."

His shoulders drooped. "But there don't seem to be any jobs like that around. I've got to figure out some way to feed my family, whether I like the work or not."

Paul nodded. "You're right. It's your responsibility to care for the family God's entrusted to you. Speaking of which, have you told your wife yet that you're unemployed?"

The way Daniel studied the glass in his hands and refused to raise his eyes gave Paul the answer.

When Daniel spoke, his voice was tight. "I can't. I've tried to lead up to it two or three times now. But every time I get started, she looks at me with those big blue eyes all full of trust and hope, and it's like something dies inside me.

"Here she's dependin' on me, and all I'm doin' is lettin' her down . . . again."

He chewed on his lower lip and stared out the office window. "What kind of man am I? It's gettin' so I can hardly stand to look at myself in the mirror."

"Guilt will do that to you," Paul said. "Your load is getting too heavy for you, and you're still trying to carry it all alone."

Daniel clenched his fists. "Well, I can't exactly ask Crystal to carry it with me."

"That's not what I meant." Paul uncrossed his legs and leaned forward. "Do you know what the biggest need in your life is?"

The younger man gave a bitter laugh. "Yeah, to find a job and take care of my family and act like a real man for once in my life."

Paul nodded. "Yes, that's the greatest earthly need. But believe it or not, there's something you need even more. Nothing will bring you the peace and hope you need like a relationship with God."

Daniel looked at Paul with a look of defiance in his eyes. "How's that gonna help me feed my wife and kids?

Are you tellin' me that if I turn my life over to God, it's
gonna make all my problems go away?"

Paul chuckled. "It would be nice if it worked out that
way, but I can't promise you it will.

"There are always going to be difficulties of one sort or
another. Some big, some small. God doesn't promise to
make them disappear, but he does promise to walk
through the hard times with you."

He could see Daniel's interest quicken.

"You mean like a friend?"

"That's right. He can be your best friend."

Daniel kept silent for several moments, then set the
glass back on Paul's blotter. He planted his hands on his
knees and pushed himself to his feet.

"I don't know, Pastor. I'd like to believe that, but my
daddy always told me that if somethin' sounds too good to
be true, it probably is. I'm gonna have to give that one
some thought."

WHEN KATE WALKED INTO the outer office, she could hear
Paul's voice on the other side of his door. Knowing that he
kept the door shut during the summer months to save on
the air-conditioning bills, she assumed he was on the
phone. Then she heard a different voice respond.

Kate stopped just outside the door and listened a
moment. It wasn't a voice she recognized.

She hesitated. Should she stay or leave? She didn't
want anyone to think she was eavesdropping, but she
really did need the Newcombs' address.

Paul spoke again. "Let me urge you to give faith a great deal of thought, Daniel. It's the most important decision you'll ever make."

Kate nearly laughed out loud. So it *was* Daniel in there with Paul!

She didn't believe in coincidences, calling them God encounters instead. How like God to bring her there at that exact moment. If she waited a few minutes, she could get directions from Daniel himself.

And it looked like she wouldn't have to wait long. Kate heard footsteps on the other side of the door, and the knob rattled.

She stepped back and waited for the knob to turn.

Instead, she heard Daniel's voice much clearer this time.

"You said something about guilt a minute ago."

She heard Paul respond, but she couldn't make out the words.

"There's somethin' more I need to talk to you about," Daniel said. "It's been eatin' away at me for weeks."

After a long pause, he continued. "Isn't there some kind of legal thing where if I tell you something, you have to keep it in confidence?"

"That depends." Paul's voice sounded closer.

Kate thought he must have walked across the room to join Daniel.

"There are some things of a criminal nature that I'm bound by law to report. You need to be aware of that before you say anything."

It was time to leave. Kate knew that whatever Daniel said next wasn't intended for her ears. She still needed that address, but whom could she ask?

Kate tiptoed over to Millie's desk, hoping to find a neighborhood directory. She flipped through as quickly as she could without making noise and tried to tune out the conversation taking place in Paul's office.

A moment later, she had the information she needed and was headed to her Accord. Even though she'd tried not to listen to what Daniel was saying, the words she did overhear set her sleuthing instincts on high alert.

Kate started the car and pulled out of the church parking lot. Now she had a dual purpose for her visit. If her suspicions were correct, Crystal Newcomb would need friends now more than ever.

Chapter Twenty-Two

The houses grew sparse as Kate drove west on Barnhill Street, then they petered out altogether. Two miles farther, she came across a row of rundown homes.

The fourth one—the Newcombs'—was the only house that bore any signs of life. The yard boasted a modest garden filled with bright summer flowers, and a tire swing hung from a tall oak tree. But the house itself looked as if it was sinking into the ground on which it stood. The paint was severely chipped, the concrete drive was splitting, and the shutterless windows were cracked in several places.

Kate's heart went out to Crystal. The distance to town wasn't too far for a healthy young woman to travel on foot from time to time, but not with two little ones in tow. And in a house like that, cabin fever was probably a daily reality for Crystal.

Kate slowed to make the turn into the driveway. If the houses nearby had been occupied, Crystal would at least have been able to visit with her neighbors. As it was, with

Daniel using their only vehicle, she spent her days in virtual isolation.

When Kate pulled into the driveway and stopped, a towheaded little boy appeared from around the far corner of the house. He stared at Kate, then dashed back to where he'd come from. A moment later he reappeared, leading a young woman carrying a little girl on her right hip.

Kate studied the trio as she got out of the car. The woman had curly black hair, pulled back from her face with a band of fabric that matched her bright print blouse. The little girl's hair was dark like her mother's, and they both had the same startling blue eyes. All three smiled as they approached Kate's Honda.

"Hi," the woman called. "Can I help you?"

"I'm looking for Crystal Newcomb," Kate began, trying to reconcile this cheery young mother with the careworn figure of her imagination.

"That's me." Crystal shifted the little girl to her left arm so she could shake Kate's hand. "This is my son, Grady." She indicated the grinning boy with a nod of her head.

"And this"—she ticked the little girl under the chin, bringing forth a giggle—"is Hannah."

"I'm Kate Hanlon. My husband is the pastor of Faith Briar Church over on Mountain Laurel Road."

Crystal nodded. "I don't get into town much, but I think I know where that is."

"How long have you lived here?" Kate asked.

"It's been about a year now. We moved here just before Grady turned three."

"I'm almost four now," Grady said proudly.

"Oh my!" Kate said with a laugh.

To Crystal, she said, "Well, please consider this a belated welcome to Copper Mill. Here, I brought something for you." She opened the passenger door of her Honda.

Grady's eyes lit up when he saw the plate of cookies. "Are those for us?"

"They are." Kate laughed again. "But you'll have to ask your mom how many you can have."

"That's so nice of you!" Crystal said. "Let's take them inside, and we'll have a tea party. What do you think, kids?"

"Just a minute." Kate set the cookies on the hood, then reached back inside the car, this time bringing out the crayons, coloring books, and stuffed animals.

"Puppy!" Hannah squealed, stretching out her arms.

"Actually, they're bears," Kate chuckled. She handed one to the little girl. "But I suppose it can be a puppy if you want it to be."

Crystal looked at her daughter fondly. "That's probably what she'll call it. She loves dogs."

Kate's pulse quickened, but she passed the other bear and the coloring materials to Grady without comment.

"Do you have time to come inside?" Crystal asked. "I was serious about that tea party. We don't get much company way out here."

Kate picked up the plate of cookies. "I'd love to."

Crystal's smile lit up her whole face. "Great. Come on in."

Kate studied the living room when they entered,

amazed to find it a sunny, inviting space. Though the outside of the house showed the ravages of time and neglect,
the inside was bright and appealing.

"You can put the cookies on that coffee table if you
like." Crystal nodded toward the table, then set Hannah
on the floor and gave her a loving pat.

The little girl toddled off to one corner of the room,
babbling to her new "puppy."

"You have two beautiful children," Kate said.

"They're the joy of my life." Crystal's pride was evident
as she stared after Hannah. "Go ahead and have a seat.
I've got sun tea in the fridge. I'll pour some for us."

While she was gone, Kate surveyed the room. The furniture looked like it had come from discount houses and
yard sales, but the room itself was clean and tidy, with
everything in its place.

A half-finished cross-stitch project lay across the arm
of an easy chair. Kate rose and went to look at it more
closely.

"I'm making that for the kids' room." Crystal returned
carrying a tray with four plates, two tall glasses of iced tea,
a smaller glass filled with lemonade, and a sippy cup that
Kate assumed was filled with lemonade as well.

She set the tray beside the cookies and held the
needlework up so Kate could see it better. "It's a Precious
Moments design. I just love those, don't you?"

In the stitched scene, two children sat playing in the
grass, while a third figure with a halo and wings hovered
above them.

"A guardian angel for my two little angels," she said with a soft smile.

Kate resumed her seat on the couch. "When do you get the time to work on something like that with two little ones around?"

Crystal chuckled. "I try to clean the house and do the yard work while they're awake. They help me a lot. Don't you?" she asked Grady, who was reaching for a chocolate-fudge-oatmeal cookie.

Grady stuffed a bite of the cookie in his mouth and grinned.

"When they go down for their naps, that's when I have time for myself. I work on my cross-stitch or read a book, things like that." She spoke without the least trace of resentment.

Kate set a chocolate-dipped peanut-butter ball on her plate and marveled. She had been prepared to offer friendship to a lonely woman beaten down by circumstances and on the verge of leaving her husband. Instead, she'd found a vibrant, charming person who seemed perfectly satisfied with her life.

While Crystal obviously enjoyed having a visitor, she also seemed like one of those rare beings who was content with her own company. Doubt flickered in Kate's mind. Had her other assumption been equally off the mark?

She sipped her tea. "Delicious!"

"It's the mint," Crystal told her. "I've got a patch growing on the shady side of the house. I put a sprig of it in the jar while the sun tea's brewing. Really peps it up, doesn't it?"

"Definitely." Kate took another sip and set down her glass. "Well, Crystal, part of the reason I came today was to invite you to a Friendship Club some ladies in our church have started. The idea is simply for women in the community to get together each week and enjoy each other's company."

Hannah tugged on her mother's shorts, and Crystal pulled the little girl into her lap and handed her the sippy cup. "That's a great idea."

"I think so too," Kate agreed. "It seems like everyone gets so busy these days, we all wind up going our separate ways. It's easy to get disconnected."

"I think I'd enjoy something like that," Crystal said. "Not that I don't have enough company with these two." She nuzzled her nose against Hannah's neck. "But it would be nice to have some women friends to talk to once in a while. I'd be glad to come if I had a car."

Kate smiled. "They're having a meeting today at three. If you'd like to go, I'd be more than happy to take you. There's someone to watch the children, so they're welcome to come along."

Crystal's eyes sparkled. "Really? That might work. If I put the kids down for a nap right now, they should be rested enough by then."

"That's wonderful!" Kate beamed, relieved to know that at least one part of her mission had come together.

"Would you like me to stay and visit, or would you rather I leave now and come back to pick you up? We can do whatever works best for—"

Loud scratching raked against a door at the far end of the room, followed by a faint whimper. Kate's heart skipped a beat.

"That's my new puppy," Crystal said with an apologetic smile.

"Be quiet, Rambo," Grady called in a stern tone.

The whimpering began again. This time Hannah mimicked her brother. "Kite, 'Bo."

Crystal giggled. "I'm sorry he's so noisy. He just isn't used to being locked up."

Kate seized the opening. "Well, if you've locked him in there for me, don't worry about it. I'd love to meet him!"

"I don't know." Crystal wrinkled her nose. "He's a sweetheart, but he gets a little excited sometimes. I don't want him to jump up on you and ruin those nice slacks." She looked toward the door. "Rambo, hush. We have company."

Instead of subsiding, the scratching grew more frantic. This time it was accompanied by a series of high-pitched barks.

Kate drew a sharp breath and pressed her hand against her chest.

Misunderstanding the gesture, Crystal set Hannah on the floor and stood. "I'm so sorry. I'll go shush him."

"No, wait. Please let him out."

Crystal stared at Kate as if trying to see whether she was serious.

"Well, if you say so." She crossed the room and pushed the door open.

Immediately, a tan, pint-sized blur burst out of the bedroom. Kate's heart stopped, then raced as a tiny, bug-eyed dog with oversized, floppy ears and a sparkly collar shot across the room straight toward her.

He skidded to a stop at Kate's feet, then danced in circles, barking wildly.

Crystal clapped her hands to her cheeks. "What on earth has gotten into him? I've never seen him act like that before."

Kate reached down and scooped the little dog into her arms. His tiny tail beat in frantic rhythm against her elbow.

"Oh my" was all Kate could say.

She held the diminutive dog out in front of her. "Kisses?"

Crystal tilted her head to one side and crinkled her forehead. "Kiss him? Well, I guess if you want to . . ."

Kate could find no more words to say. She simply reveled in the joy of the moment as Kisses wriggled in her arms, his little pink tongue planting doggy smooches on her cheek.

The lost had at last been found.

"This is Rambo?" Kate asked.

"Uh-huh. It's kind of a silly name for a dog that size, I guess. But Grady picked it out, so we decided to go along with it."

"I see." Kate studied Crystal, who still stood at the open door, looking utterly astonished by her "puppy's" behavior.

Astonished, but not on edge. Kate saw no guarded air, no telltale sign of guilt on the other woman's face. It was all too obvious that Crystal had no idea her new dog had been stolen from someone else.

Sadness washed over Kate, tempering her elation at finding Kisses. She had come out to catch a perpetrator, and instead she had found another victim.

How was she going to break the news to Crystal?

Kate stroked the top of Kisses' head as she had seen Renee do countless times. "I'm not sure how to tell you this," she began.

The front door swung open, and Kate heard a voice call out, "Hon, I've gotta talk to you."

Chapter Twenty-Three

Kate turned to see a slender, sandy-haired man framed in the doorway. He stared back, taking in the sight of her holding Kisses with something like horror in his eyes.

Over his shoulder, she could see Paul. When his eyes met Kate's, she knew he shared the mingled sense of joy and sadness she was feeling.

"Daniel," Paul said, "this is my wife, Kate."

Without taking his eyes off her and the little dog, Daniel moved across the room to stand beside his wife.

Crystal slipped her arm around his waist and looked up at him. "Would you please tell me what's going on?"

Daniel raked his fingers through his hair. "We'd better sit down. This is going to take a while."

Crystal took a long look at him. "Give me a minute to put the kids down first." She picked up Hannah, then took Grady by the hand and led him toward a bedroom at the back of the house.

She returned a few moments later and joined Daniel on the couch. She reached over and took both of his hands in hers. "Okay, tell me what this is all about."

Daniel drew in a deep breath and turned to face her. "I need to tell you I've been talkin' to the preacher quite a bit lately. The good news is that I decided today that it's time to get right with God."

Kate shot a startled glance at Paul. He smiled and nodded but didn't say anything.

"I need to start doin' things different," Daniel said. "First of all, I've gotta be honest with you."

Some of the color left Crystal's face. "What do you mean?"

Daniel took in another breath and let out a shuddering sigh. "I lost my job."

"Again?" Crystal regarded him thoughtfully, then lifted one hand to smooth the hair back from his forehead. "Well, we've made it through tight times before, so I guess we can do it again."

Daniel wrapped his arms around his wife and buried his face in her neck. "I love you, Crystal. You're the best."

"That's what I keep telling you," she said in a teasing tone. "So, that's your bad news?"

Daniel's face fell. "Not all of it. The other part's about Rambo."

Kate looked at Paul, and he mouthed, "Rambo?"

Crystal's face crinkled in confusion. "My puppy? What about him?"

Daniel clenched his fists on his knees and squeezed his eyes shut. "He isn't yours, hon. Not really."

"I don't get it. What do you mean he's not mine?"

Daniel sagged against the back of the threadbare

couch and stared at the opposite wall. "Do you remember just before your birthday how I promised we'd have a big celebration, and I'd do somethin' to make it real special for you?"

"And you did," Crystal said with a dreamy smile. "It was my best birthday ever."

Daniel's face tightened. "Well, just after I made you that promise, I got fired."

Crystal's eyes grew round. "That was weeks ago! Why didn't you tell me? What have you been doing all this time?"

"Doin' odd jobs, lookin' for work, and talkin' to the preacher." Daniel rubbed one hand across the back of his neck.

"But, anyway, about your birthday. Here I told you I was goin' to do somethin' really fine, and then I didn't have the money to follow through on it.

"I'd seen you lookin' at that white purse at the Mercantile a couple of times. You know the one I mean?"

Crystal nodded. "The one with all the little pockets and places to sort things." Her face lit up. "You noticed?"

"Yeah, I did. I went back on your birthday to get it. I wanted to do so much more for you, but I figured I could buy you at least one thing I knew you really liked. But when I checked the price, it came down to a choice between buyin' the purse or groceries for the week."

Kate's heart ached as she pictured Daniel having to choose between feeding his family or buying his wife a simple birthday gift.

"I knew I'd have to come clean about bein' fired eventually," Daniel went on, "but I just couldn't bear the thought of ruinin' your birthday with news like that. I wanted to get you somethin' so bad, it hurt. But I didn't know what I was gonna do."

Daniel scrubbed his cheek with his hand. "I bought the groceries, but it was too early to come straight home, so I decided to drive around town a bit. I was passing Copper Mill Park, and I spotted a bag that looked just like the one in the Mercantile."

It took an effort for Kate to hold back a laugh. Only a man without an ounce of fashion sense could mistake one of Sam's stock purses for a designer doggie tote! Both bags were white, but the similarity ended there.

"I stopped the Blazer and looked around. It was just sittin' there like someone had gone off and left it. The more I looked at it, the more I knew you had to have it."

No one broke the silence when Daniel paused and stared down at his hands.

"I looked around and saw these two old ladies. I figured the bag must have belonged to one of them. I waited there for a bit to see if they were gonna come back for it. Then they walked over to a bench and sat down, and I saw my chance."

"Oh no," Crystal whispered.

Daniel hung his head. "Yeah, I kept the trees between me and those ladies and sneaked up close to the bag. Then I grabbed it and took off."

"You stole my birthday present?"

Daniel nodded miserably. "It was wrong. It was stupid. I can see that now. But by the time I let myself think about it, it was too late to do anythin'. I was gonna sneak it in the house and gift wrap it when I got home, but then you came out on the porch and caught me before I could get inside."

"I remember." A soft light shone in Crystal's eyes. "There was that beautiful bag, and when I looked inside and saw that precious puppy staring up at me, I felt like a little girl at Christmas. It was the most wonderful surprise."

"Yeah," Daniel said. "I was about as surprised as you were when I first saw that dog."

"Wait a minute," Paul interrupted. "You mean you didn't know there was a dog in the bag? Surely you must have realized something was in there when you picked it up."

"I knew there was something, but I didn't bother looking inside." Daniel managed a half smile. "That dog can't weigh more than a few pounds. Knowin' how much ladies can cram inside their purses, I didn't think much about it. I just figured I'd empty it out before I wrapped it when I got home. But on the way home, the bag started to wiggle, and this little guy started whimperin'. I knew then that I had gotten more than I bargained for, but it was too late to go back."

Crystal sent a longing look across the room, where Kisses was nestled in Kate's arms. "I fell in love with Rambo the moment I laid eyes on him. He's so tiny and cute. It's like having another baby to hold."

"That's why I couldn't tell you about the gift or the job, hon. I just couldn't stand the thought of wipin' that joy off your face."

Daniel propped his elbows on his knees and buried his face in his hands. "But it looks like I've gone and done it now."

Tires crunched on the driveway. Daniel's head jerked up, and he looked at Paul. "Is he here?"

Paul glanced out the window and nodded. "Shall I let him in?"

"Might as well get it over with." Daniel looked at his wife. "Sweetheart, I meant it when I said I got things straight between me and God today. If I'm gonna do this right, I've gotta do it all the way."

A quick tap sounded at the door. At Daniel's nod, Paul opened it, and Skip Spencer stepped into the room.

Crystal gasped and covered her mouth with both hands.

Daniel stood and gathered her into his arms. "Don't worry, honey. I'm the one who oughta be scared, not you."

Crystal's chin quivered as she looked up at him. "Why?"

Daniel pressed her head tight against his chest. "I can't expect you and the kids to get by on your own if they put me in jail for this."

His voice thickened. "I just want you to know that if you feel like you have to pack up and go back home to your mom and dad, I'll understand."

Crystal flung her arms around his neck. "Don't you

know me better than that by now? I love you, Daniel Blaine Newcomb, and I'll stand by you, whatever happens."

Daniel's face twisted with emotion. "But you gotta eat somehow."

She lifted her chin in a show of bravery that tugged at Kate's heart. "I was a checker at the grocery store before the kids were born, remember? If I have to, I can do it again. I'm sure I can find someone to watch them."

Skip stepped across to the couple, and he and Daniel began speaking in low tones.

Kate drew away and moved over beside Paul. "How did Skip know about this?" she whispered.

Paul reached out and ran his forefinger between Kisses' ears. The tip of the little Chihuahua's tail quivered.

Paul lowered his voice to match hers. "That was Daniel's doing. He's been wrestling with a load of guilt for a long time, and he finally realized that the only way to get rid of it was to own up to what he'd done and face the consequences.

"He asked if I'd follow him out here for moral support, but he didn't give me the specifics of what he'd stolen until we got to the house. Before we came in, he borrowed my cell phone to call Skip and asked him to meet us here.

"He knows it's going to cost him, but he said he wants to be able to stand up and know he faced it like a real man."

Paul looked at the young man with respect in his eyes. "I'd say he's serious about this commitment he made to follow God. It took a lot of courage to do what he did."

"It did indeed." Kate looked across the living room to

where Skip and Daniel were still deep in conversation with Crystal staying next to Daniel's side. Both men's faces wore solemn expressions. She felt her stomach tighten and wondered how this was going to end.

She tucked one hand under Paul's arm and leaned against his shoulder, careful not to squeeze Kisses between them. "It was quite a surprise to have Daniel come in the door like that and then see you standing behind him."

Paul chuckled. "How do you think I felt when I saw your car sitting in the driveway? I thought I was finally going to solve a mystery ahead of you, and you'd already beaten me to it!"

Kate shook her head. "It was the oddest thing. I came into Millie's office while you and Daniel were talking. Did you know anybody was there?"

"No, I never heard you." Paul grinned. "I'll have to be more careful what I say if you're able to sneak up on me like that."

Kate pulled her hand free and gave him a light punch on the shoulder. "I'd lost the Newcombs' address and stopped by to get it from you. When I realized you were talking to Daniel, I decided to wait. But then I overheard Daniel talking about making some kind of confession, and I knew it was time to go. But I'd heard enough to suspect what I might find once I got here."

Paul looked at her with a twinkle in his eyes. "That sounds like divine intervention to me."

"I think we're about ready to wrap this up." Skip spoke loud enough for all of them to hear. "I'm going to need that tote."

Crystal went into the bedroom Kisses had occupied and returned with the white designer tote in her hands. She pulled out a worn wallet, a tube of lip gloss, and a comb, then held it out to Skip. "Here it is. I've taken good care of it. It isn't scratched or anything."

Skip took the tote and nodded his thanks.

Crystal clung to Daniel's arm and gazed at Kisses, who was still nestled in Kate's arms. "I guess that means I have to give Rambo back too, doesn't it?"

Daniel wrapped his arm around her waist. "Don't worry, hon. When all of this is behind us, we'll go out and buy another dog. I've been thinkin' about a coonhound."

Kate stepped forward. "I know his owner, Renee Lambert, will appreciate the care you've given her dog. It's easy to tell he's been treated well. You probably don't know this, but she entered him in a dog show this coming Saturday here in Copper Mill. He'll probably still be able to compete because of your loving care."

Crystal sniffed. "I guess everything works out in the end. I've really loved having him here, and it's been a joy to care for him."

"It doesn't look like the change has put him off his feed," Kate said.

"Nah," Daniel said. "He isn't picky. I just bought the cheap stuff up at SuperMart. He liked it fine."

Kate tilted her head to look at Kisses, the finicky soul who wouldn't touch anything but the food that Renee prepared from scratch three times a day.

"Do you want me to get the bag of food?" Crystal asked. "There's still plenty left. I could send it home with him."

Kate swallowed, thinking of Renee's probable reaction. "That's okay. Save it for when you get your coonhound."

Crystal sniffled again and nodded. She turned to Skip. "What's going to happen to my husband? You aren't going to have to take him out of here in handcuffs, are you?"

"No, I don't see any reason for that. We're not talking about a violent crime here. He turned himself in, and he's being cooperative. I'll just need to take him to Pine Ridge to see the justice of the peace and find out where we go from there."

Daniel's face grew taut. "Do you think it's going to mean jail time?"

Skip considered the question. "It isn't for me to say, but I doubt it. Seeing as how you've taken the initiative on this, I'm thinking he'll probably lean toward giving you community service."

Skip stepped toward the door and gestured to Daniel. "We'd better get going."

Crystal wrapped her arms around Daniel's waist and hugged him tight. "Just remember, the kids and I will be here for you, no matter what."

"Wait a minute, Skip. When will Renee get Kisses and her tote back?" Kate asked.

"Well, the tote is evidence," Skip said. "I'll have to keep it for a while, at least until after I see what the judge says.

"As far as Kisses is concerned . . ." He looked at the bug-eyed little dog. "Why don't you follow us to my office? I'll need to take a picture of him. Then you can take him home to Miz Lambert."

"THAT'S THE FIRST TIME I ever witnessed a doggy mug shot being taken." Paul chuckled as he opened the driver's-side door of the Honda for Kate. They had decided to leave Paul's truck at the Town Hall and pick it up on their way home after dropping Kisses off at Renee's.

He helped Kate into the car and then he trotted around to the passenger side and climbed in, pulling Kisses onto his lap. "This time you're sharing the seat, buddy."

"Yes, Kisses, but as soon as things are back to normal, you'll be riding in your place of honor again in your favorite pink Olds," Kate promised.

Her spirits soared as she started the car. She could hardly wait to see Renee's face when Kisses made his triumphal return.

"Look at this." Paul pointed at Kisses, who stood on his back legs in Paul's lap. His front paws rested on the window ledge, and his tiny nose was pressed against the glass.

Kate felt tears sting her eyes. "It's like he knows he's going home."

"Hang on, fella," Paul told Kisses as they headed down Euclid. "It won't be long now."

"What do you think?" he asked as Kate made a right turn onto Main. "Is he going to miss being at the Newcombs'?"

Kate shot a startled glance his way. "After being cosseted and treated like a king at Renee's? Are you kidding?"

"I don't know," Paul teased. "Think about his male ego.

For more than three weeks, he's been treated like a real dog. And with a manly name like Rambo, no less. It's going to make for quite a transition, going back to being Little Umpkins."

"You may have a point," Kate laughed. "I guess we'll just have to wait and see."

She made a left on Smith, then a right on Ashland and pulled up in front of Renee's house on the corner.

"I feel like there should be a brass band playing," she said when she got out of the car.

"A ticker-tape parade at the very least," Paul agreed.

Kisses squirmed so much that he nearly wriggled out of Paul's grasp.

"Hang on there, buddy," Paul said. "Just a couple more minutes."

Kate grinned. "So much for him turning up his nose at the idea of being cosseted."

She pressed the doorbell and heard it chime inside the house. Paul stood beside her, with Kisses in full view.

The door opened almost immediately, and Renee breathed a sigh of relief as soon as she saw them. "Oh, Kate, I'm glad you're here. I want you to help me proof-read a letter I'm writing to the editor of *Teacup* magazine. I'm urging all owners of small breeds to—"

Kisses yipped. Renee stopped short with her mouth wide open, seeming to register the wriggling dog in Paul's arms for the first time.

She put her hand on the door frame to steady herself. "Oh my stars. Is it really him this time?"

Kisses whimpered, then yipped again.

"My little baby! Come to Mommy!" Renee reached out, and Kisses leaped straight into her waiting arms.

Thank You, Lord, Kate prayed as tears welled up in her eyes.

"I STILL CAN'T BELIEVE IT," Renee said for the umpteenth time.

Paul and Kate sat on overstuffed chairs in the living room. Renee and her mother occupied the couch. Kisses lay curled up in Renee's lap as if he'd never been gone.

Renee ran her hand down his sleek tan coat and shook her head. "I can't get over it. I had such horrible thoughts running through my mind all the time he was gone. I expected him to be half starved, but he doesn't look like he's been mistreated at all."

She stroked his side with her clipped fingernail. "I do believe he's put on a bit of weight. Can you believe that?"

Paul smirked, and Kate raised one eyebrow in warning.

"In fact," Renee added, "he looks so good I think I may be able to put him in the show on Saturday after all. I'm sure all his doggie friends will be overjoyed to see him."

Kate smiled. "I'm sure they will."

Renee turned to Paul. "And you say the man who took my tote didn't even realize Kisses was inside?"

"Not at first. He didn't discover Kisses until he was on his way home with the tote. He isn't a bad person at heart," Paul added. "He just felt like life had backed him into a corner. It was more an act of desperation than any-thing. He took the tote as a gift for his wife's birthday."

"Well, at least they took good care of my Little Umpkins."

"They certainly did," Kate assured her. "Both the cou-ple and their children adored him."

Renee's eyes misted over. "A sensitive dog like Kisses needs to know he's treasured and loved. It's a necessity—not superfluous pampering—no matter what some people might say."

She sniffled, and Kate knew that the sting of Lucy Mae's comments at the beauty parlor hadn't gone away entirely, even though the two women had reconciled.

Renee held the Chihuahua up and placed a kiss on the top of his little domed head. "You're home safe and sound now, and that's all that matters. And Mommy is going to make sure you're never left alone again."

Chapter Twenty-Four

"Tell me again what it is you're supposed to be doin' on Saturday?" LuAnne asked as she leaned against the Hanlons' kitchen counter on Thursday evening.

Livvy stood beside LuAnne with an equally bemused expression on her face. "I'd like to know too, since I'm supposed to be helping you. It would be a big plus if I had some clue about what it is I volunteered for."

"An offer that is *much* appreciated, believe me." Kate laughed and greased another cookie sheet. "All I know is what I've been told—greet people, see that they have everything they need, and take care of small problems that come up."

She shrugged off the niggling doubts that the mention of "small problems" always brought on. "Whatever happens, Paul keeps reminding me that by Saturday night, it'll all be over."

Livvy grinned. "Making people welcome ought to be second nature to you after so many years of greeting people on Sunday mornings."

"So what are the cookies for?" LuAnne asked.

Kate followed LuAnne's gaze to the counter, which was piled high with an array of cookies: chocolate-chip, oatmeal-raisin, lemon snowballs, and snickerdoodles.

Kate had even made sugar cookies in the shape of little hound dogs. She hoped the owners of other breeds wouldn't take that as an indication of favoritism. It was the only dog-shaped cookie cutter she owned.

She grinned. "Maybe it's all those years of church potlucks, but hospitality is always connected in my mind with food. I thought I'd set up a table with trays of cookies and jugs of iced tea. Maybe a coffee urn, if I can find a place in the park to plug one in."

"That ought to set a nice tone when people arrive," Livvy said.

"Nothin' says welcome like something from the kitchen," LuAnne agreed.

Kate peeked in the oven to check the progress of her latest batch, then she closed the door to give it a few more minutes.

LuAnne wrinkled her nose. "I can't believe you're making cookies for the dogs too."

Kate felt her face flame and hoped her friends would attribute her pink cheeks to the heat from the oven. Even she wondered if she might be going a little over the top with that idea. Maybe Renee was rubbing off on her.

"I came across the recipe in that dog magazine, and I figured this would be the perfect time to give it a try." She set bone-shaped pieces of dough onto a cookie sheet, ready to pop into the oven when the first batch of doggie treats was finished.

"I know it seems crazy to heat up the house like this when the weather is so miserable, but this baking frenzy has been therapeutic for me. I've been so concerned the past few weeks about Kisses and Renee. Now that Kisses is home again, I needed to do something to use up my excess energy."

LuAnne surveyed the profusion of baked goodies. "From the looks of things, you've burned up plenty of energy today. You'd better conserve a little bit for Saturday."

"Have you heard any more about the guy who took Kisses?" Livvy asked.

"Not yet. Daniel is really a nice young man, in spite of what he did. I hope he doesn't get in too much trouble over it."

LuAnne snorted. "After all the heartache he caused Renee?"

"I know. I felt that way too, at first." Kate pushed damp strands of hair off her forehead with the back of her hand. "After I overheard what he said in Paul's office and had a pretty good idea he was the dognapper, and after dealing with the Murphys, I assumed his wife might be in on it too. I started out to their house, ready to convict them. But once I met his family and found out why he took the tote, I saw things a little differently. In a way, what he did was rather sweet. Inexcusable, but sweet."

She opened the oven door again to check on the doggie treats.

LuAnne sniffed and gave Kate a suspicious glance. "What did you put in those things?"

"Wheat germ, powdered milk, brewer's yeast, and pureed liver. It sounded very healthy."

LuAnne exchanged a long look with Livvy. "Remind me not to try any of those by mistake."

"No problem," Livvy deadpanned. "Just make sure you don't reach for anything that's shaped like a bone."

The doorbell sounded.

"Would one of you mind getting that?" Kate asked as she donned her oven mitt.

While Livvy went off to answer the door, Kate pulled the doggie treats out of the oven.

Livvy returned with Renee and Kisses in tow.

Kate slid the bone-shaped morsels onto a cooling rack and walked over to rub her finger behind Kisses' ears.

He looked up and gave her a doggie grin.

"How's the prodigal pooch?" LuAnne asked.

Renee drew herself up. "I would remind you that the prodigal son left home of his own accord. In Kisses' case, it was hardly by choice."

Then she dropped her show of pique and looked down at Kisses as if she still couldn't believe he was back with her again.

"He's doing fine. I had Dr. Milt give Kisses a thorough examination on Tuesday just to make sure he hadn't suffered any ill effects from being abducted."

"He must be quite a resilient little guy," Livvy said.

Renee nodded happily. "In fact, Dr. Milt told me on

Tuesday that Kisses is in even better condition than at his last checkup. He said the same thing when we saw him again this afternoon."

Renee narrowed her eyes down to slits, then she waved her hand. "Surely he was exaggerating."

"So why did you go back today, if everything was fine?" LuAnne asked.

"I'm worried about him." Renee lifted Kisses and rubbed her cheek against the top of his head. "I can't put my finger on it, but I feel that something is wrong."

Kate studied the little dog. "Like what?"

"He just isn't acting like himself. His appetite seems to have changed, for one thing. I fixed him his usual ground meat, garlic, and onions, and he hardly touched it. He took a few bites, then he backed away and turned up his nose at the rest."

"Let's see what he thinks about these." LuAnne reached over and snagged one of the bone-shaped doggie treats. Breaking off a corner, she held it on her palm and offered it to Kisses.

He sniffed at it tentatively, then reached out and gobbled it up. He smacked his tongue and sniffed LuAnne's hand as if looking for more.

"See there?" Renee's voice wobbled. "That isn't anything like his usual fare at all. And yesterday, I found him digging into a bag of trash I had sitting out ready to take to the curb for collection."

Worry lines creased her forehead. "He'd torn a hole in the side of the bag and had his head wedged inside the hole. He was . . . rooting around in the trash like a common mongrel."

Her voice caught. "I'm wondering if he's had some sort of psychological trauma."

Kate bit her lip and turned as if to put the oven mitt away so the others wouldn't see the merriment on her face. Maybe she should suggest Renee go buy a bag of the cheapest dog food SuperMart had to offer.

Then again, maybe not.

She smoothed her face into a compassionate expression. "Give him a few days. I'm sure he'll return to his normal, happy self in no time.

"Are you still planning for him to compete in the show?" Kate asked.

The older woman beamed. "I am indeed. Physically, he's fine, and he looks absolutely beautiful. I'm sure he'll do very well."

Kate couldn't help but notice that Renee had toned down her earlier predictions of victory.

Kate handed Kisses another treat. "I'm sure he'll have a fine time," she told Renee. "It should be a lovely day."

Chapter Twenty-Five

W here's that pin brush?"

"I'll be with you in a minute." Kate pulled a coiled extension cord from under the hospitality table.

"I need the brush *now*." A stocky, red-faced woman planted her hands on the table and leaned across it toward Kate. "My shih tzu's class will be coming up soon."

Kate pushed the extension cord toward the woman and pulled the lid off the plastic crate at her feet.

Velma Hopkins had brought the crate by while Kate was arranging refreshments on the hospitality table early that morning. "This is our just-in-case box," Velma had informed Kate. "Brushes, combs, palm pads, lint rollers, that sort of thing. There's always someone who arrives at the show without some bit of equipment they need, and then it becomes an emergency."

The woman standing in front of Kate let out an impatient huff.

Kate lowered herself gingerly on her arthritic knee and scrabbled through the jumble in the crate, realizing that over the course of the day, it had been nearly emptied of its supplies.

"We need more bottled water for the judges," an official near the ring shouted.

Kate pulled out a wooden-handled brush that reminded her of a pin cushion and held it up. "Is this what you're looking for?"

The woman grabbed it and took off without a word of thanks.

Kate grimaced as she pushed herself upright and opened a nearby ice chest, also delivered by Velma at the beginning of the day.

Livvy bustled up to the table. "I took the forced-air dryer to the man with the Newfoundland. What's next?"

Kate pulled four ice-cold bottles of spring water from the chest and thrust them into Livvy's hands. "Take these over to the ring, please. And Livvy?"

Her friend paused, and Kate reached out to give her a quick hug. "Thanks for volunteering to help. I don't know what I would have done without you."

Livvy gave her a wink. "Glad to help. What's Sherlock without her Watson?"

"Mrs. Hanlon?"

Livvy smiled, then trotted off, and Kate turned to see Wilbur Dodson standing before her.

"Hello, there. What can I do for you?" She had to fight the urge to reach out to tweak his ever-present bow tie back into its usual precise alignment. How anyone could stand to wear a buttoned-up collar in this sweltering heat was beyond her.

Wilbur stood erect with both hands behind his back. "I'd like to congratulate you. Things seem to be running along quite smoothly, due in large part to your efforts. Thank you . . . uh . . . for throwing yourself into the spirit of things in such a . . . wholehearted way."

Kate leaned against the hospitality table, partly from exhaustion and partly to keep from falling over from the shock of his unsolicited compliment. "Thank you. I'm glad my friend and I have been of help."

"The refreshments were a very nice touch as well." Wilbur nodded at the table.

Kate looked down at the remains of the cookies she had labored over. Over the course of the morning and early afternoon, the plates had been picked as clean as if a horde of locusts had come through. Only crumbs remained.

Wilbur cleared his throat in the dry, raspy way he used to preface some unpleasant news. "There is one other thing."

Kate braced herself. What had she done wrong?

"The club officers were pleasantly surprised at the turnout we've had from pet owners in the area. It has brought fresh interest in the dog show, and we've seen a record number of spectators today. We're very grateful for your urging us to take this course of action."

Kate smiled and let herself relax.

"However . . ."

Kate's tension returned.

"While the experienced exhibitors are used to cleaning up after their animals, it appears that the same cannot be said of those who aren't familiar with dog-show etiquette."

He nodded toward the show area that had been set up for the unpedigreed animals. "We've had several complaints already.

"We don't want to create an unpleasant experience for the spectators. Besides, our agreement with the town of Copper Mill stipulates that we're responsible for leaving the park in the pristine condition in which we found it. If we don't, we'll be assessed a substantial cleanup fee."

Kate's shoulders sagged. "Oh dear. I had no idea. Is there anything I can do?"

"There is indeed." Wilbur brought his arms out in front of him. Kate looked down, halfway expecting to see Wilbur swing his gavel into action. Instead, she saw a roll of plastic bags in one hand and a pooper-scooper in the other.

"Here you are, Mrs. Hanlon. Happy scooping."

KATE WALKED TOWARD the show area, her cleaning equipment weighing heavy in her hands.

I don't know, Lord. Washing feet would be easy compared to this.

It was one thing to pick up after tiny Kisses when he came to visit "Grandma." But this was going to be cleanup duty on a larger scale.

Kate looked around the grassy expanse and could see Wilbur's point. Okay, a *much* larger scale.

She stepped toward the ring to watch the preparations for the costume contest while she geared up mentally for the unpleasant task ahead.

The show announcer called the names of the first pair of contenders: "Ambrose Lee and his dog, General."

Kate joined the crowd in chuckling when a stout man dressed as a Confederate soldier strode into the ring accompanied by a Great Dane in full officer's regalia, complete with plumed hat.

The laughter increased as the dogs and their owners continued to parade in, showing a wide range of creativity and humor.

Among the others, Kate noted a Jack Russell terrier dressed as a pirate, and a little girl decked out as Little Bo Peep with her white poodle portraying a woolly lamb. She smiled when the last entrant came into the ring—a bloodhound dressed as Sherlock Holmes, resplendent in deerstalker hat and flowing cape.

Kate grinned. She knew which entry she'd be rooting for.

"A penny for your thoughts," said a voice behind her.

Kate turned and gave Paul a weary smile. "I'm not sure you want to know what I'm thinking right now." She held up both hands.

Paul noted the scooper and the plastic bags. "How did you wind up with those?"

Kate made a wry face. "All part of being the hospitality chairman, apparently."

"Ouch. I guess with some jobs, the surprises never end. Are you—" Paul broke off, and a pleased smile spread across his face.

Kate looked over her shoulder and saw Daniel and

Crystal Newcomb a few yards away. Crystal was carrying Hannah on one hip and held Grady by the hand. All four of them wore smiles.

When the group reached the Hanlons, Paul reached out to shake Daniel's hand. "I didn't expect to see you here today. What brings you to the dog show?"

"Shoppin'." Daniel chuckled at Paul's startled expression and slipped his arm around Crystal's shoulder. "That's part of the reason, anyway. We figured havin' all these dogs together in one place would give us a good chance to look around and settle on the kind we really want . . . When we can afford it, of course."

Crystal poked her husband in the ribs. "And that doesn't necessarily mean a coonhound."

They all laughed. Paul looked around to make sure no one was standing nearby and lowered his voice. "How did things go with the justice of the peace?"

"Thirty hours of community service; no jail time." Daniel's face looked far more relaxed than the last time Kate had seen him. "I don't mind puttin' in the time that way, I'm just glad I didn't have to leave Crystal and the kids on their own."

Kate perked up. "Did you say community service?"

"Yeah, that's the other reason I'm here today. I'm supposed to help clean up the grounds after the show."

"In that case," Kate sighed happily and held out both hands. "I hereby bequeath these to you. And if you don't mind, you can start on this before the end of the show." She indicated the area with a sweep of her arm. "Believe me, you'll be doing a service."

Paul grinned and shook his head. "Before you get started, I just heard about a job you might want to check out. There's a campground here in Harrington County that needs a caretaker. Lots of time spent outdoors, a lot of handyman work.

"There's a small house on the grounds for the caretaker to live in, so they have someone there to keep an eye on the place even when it isn't in use. Your family could move into the place, and you'd be working on your own a lot, nobody looking over your shoulder. Are you interested?"

Daniel looked like he was ready to burst at the seams. "I'll say. That sounds like it fits me to a T."

Crystal's eyes shone. "And if we lived right where you worked, that would free up the Blazer so I can use it sometimes."

"Who do I need to talk to?" Daniel asked.

"Stop by my office on Monday morning, and I'll give you the details."

"We might just come to church tomorrow. How about if I get it from you then?"

Paul smiled. "That would be even better."

The loudspeaker crackled, and a voice invited spectators and exhibitors to gather at the main show ring for the presentation of a special award.

"Excuse me," Kate said. "I need to go see this."

Paul and Kate said their good-byes to the Newcombs and walked hand in hand across the grass to the main show area.

Kate spotted Brenna Phillips' dark hair through the crowd and waved. Brenna waved back and made her way to where they stood. When she got nearer, Kate could see the small bundle she held in her arms.

Paul grinned at the dog with the round head and floppy ears. "Hey, I remember this little guy. He looks a lot happier today than the last time I saw him."

Brenna held up the tan Chihuahua and beamed like a proud mother.

"How's he adjusting to being a part of your family?" Kate asked.

"Great. Thanks so much for talking my mom into letting me keep him! He's so small, it hardly costs anything to feed him, so if I work one day a week for Mrs. Blount during the school year, I'll be able to afford to keep him."

"That's wonderful." The joy on Brenna's face sent a warm glow through Kate. "I know how badly you've wanted a dog, and I'm so happy he's found a good home. What's his name, by the way? Have you picked one yet?"

"Yeah, his name's Ringer." The Chihuahua's tail wagged furiously, and Brenna laughed. "See? He likes it."

"Ringer," Paul repeated. "That's an interesting name."

The girl giggled. "Everybody kept saying he was a dead ringer for Mrs. Lambert's dog, so it seemed to fit."

"Is everyone having a good time?" Lawton Briddle, flanked by Lucy Mae and Micah, joined the group.

"It's been a lovely day," Kate said. "They've had a wonderful turnout, and for the most part, things have run quite smoothly." It was true, she realized with a sense of accomplishment. Despite all the hectic activity, the event had proven to be a rousing success for Copper Mill. And she had been part of it.

Lawton looked around, nodding as though he'd been personally responsible for the day's success. "This will go down as a shining moment in my tenure as mayor. I'm proud to have given it my full support."

Behind him, Lucy Mae rolled her eyes.

Kate caught the shy smile Micah gave Brenna and looked over in time to see a pink flush creep up Brenna's face.

She smothered a grin and turned to Lucy Mae. "How did Sir Percival do?"

"He won Best of Breed." Lucy Mae's voice vibrated with pride.

"That's wonderful," Kate replied. "You must be thrilled."

Out of the corner of her eye, she could see Micah step over next to Brenna. He kept his voice low, but she could make out the words over Paul and Lawton's conversation about the amount of revenue the show had brought into the community.

"My mom and stepdad just bought a new house," Micah was saying. "I'm going back to live with them next week."

"A new house? That's cool."

"Yeah." Micah looked at the ground and scuffed his foot. "Would it be okay if I write to you once I get home?"

"Sure." Brenna shrugged. "That'd be okay." She gave Micah a mischievous grin. "And I'll write you back, as long as you stay out of trouble."

Lawton's booming voice increased in volume. "The only downside to this whole day is the humidity." He took out his handkerchief and used it to mop his brow. "I've gotten several complaints about it. I kept tellin' people I'm not the one in charge of the weather."

"It's sticky, all right," Paul agreed. "It seems like it gets muggier every day."

"That's why they call these the dog days of summer," Lawton said. "It's so hot, even dogs don't want to get up and move around."

"Actually," Micah said, "the ancient Romans came up with that one. The hottest weather comes when Sirius—the Dog Star—rises and sets at the same time as the sun. They figured that was why it got so hot, so they called them the dog days."

The whole group stared at Micah in stunned silence.

Brenna smiled proudly. "He knows random things like that."

When the group shifted their gazes to her, a deep blush rose up her neck and colored her cheeks.

"There you are." Lisa walked up behind Brenna with Jeff Turner at her side.

"Hi, Lisa! How nice to see you," Kate said. "Brenna was just telling us how well Ringer is fitting into your family."

Lisa reached out to scratch the little dog behind his ears. "I have to admit he's been a lot of fun. Thanks for thinking of Brenna."

"I was happy to help," Kate said. "I'm glad it's working out for all of you."

Lisa looked at her daughter. "Better wrap things up. It's time we were going."

"Oh, right." Brenna looked at Kate. "By the way, I wanted to let you and Pastor Paul know I won't be at church tomorrow."

"Oh?"

Lisa turned to them with a light in her eyes that Kate hadn't seen before. "Jeff convinced me I need to reconcile with my parents. I called them last night."

"And?" Kate held her breath.

"The three of us are driving to Charlotte, North Carolina, to see them. We're leaving this afternoon. It'll put us there late tonight."

Kate chuckled. "You and Brenna and Ringer, eh?"

Lisa's eyes sparkled. "I guess I should have said the *four* of us: Brenna, Ringer, me . . . and Jeff." She looked up at the man standing beside her, and a dimple formed in her cheek.

Paul stared at Jeff, and his eyebrows soared to his hairline. "You're going too?"

Jeff shrugged and grinned. "We're taking my truck. I knew that car of hers would never make the trip."

Paul merely nodded, but Kate saw the corners of his mouth twitch.

"We'll see you when you get back," he said. "Have a safe trip."

Kate and Paul watched the three of them—four, counting Ringer—walk across the grass toward Jeff's truck.

No, make that five, she thought. Kate's lips curved upward when she saw Micah hurrying to catch up to say good-bye to Brenna.

THE LOUDSPEAKER CRACKLED AGAIN. One of the judges adjusted the microphone and smiled at the spectators. "We have a new award this year. It's one I've never heard of before but am pleased to present. Let me tell you a little bit about it.

"This is the Exhibitors' Choice Award. I'm sure you're all familiar with the Miss Congeniality Award given at some beauty pageants, where a contestant is given the honor by her peers. At a dog show, of course, the contestants themselves cannot make the nominations and do the voting."

She waited for the laughter to die down before she went on. "But we did ask their owners to nominate one animal who embodies the attributes that make our dogs such special creatures: courage, loyalty, and of course, friendliness to others. There's a reason dogs are known as man's best friend."

The judge smiled. "I am proud to present the first annual Exhibitors' Choice Award for the Harrington County Dog Show to ... Kisses, owned by Renee Lambert."

Kate let out a whoop and clapped wildly, pleased that the rest of the crowd was doing the same.

Renee stepped forward with Kisses in her arms. She accepted the trophy and held it up for the crowd to see, then departed to more applause.

"Exhibitors' Choice," Paul said. "Isn't that one of the ideas you came up with?"

Kate smoothed a tear from her cheek and nodded

happily. "I had no idea who was going to receive it. That was wonderful, especially after everything Renee has been through. Look, here she comes!"

"Excuse us! Winners coming through!" Renee stopped beside Kate, her arms full with Kisses and the trophy.

She looked and sounded like the old Renee, Kate noted with a vast sense of relief. That afternoon her hair was perfectly groomed, her makeup flawlessly applied, and the polish on her freshly manicured nails matched her cheery pink outfit. Kate even detected the unmistakable scent of Estée Lauder's Youth-Dew.

Kate reached out to give a hug that would encompass Renee, Kisses, and the trophy but settled for a quick one-armed squeeze around Renee's shoulders instead. "What an exciting day!"

"Congratulations!" Lucy Mae walked over and admired the trophy. "That's quite an honor for Kisses. And for you, of course."

"I'll admit I was taken aback," Renee told her. "I've always known he was the sweetest little dog, but it's nice to know that others recognize his finer qualities too. And knowing that the nomination came from other competitors . . ." Her voice caught, and she paused a moment to compose herself. "I can't tell you how much that touched me."

Renee bent to nuzzle her cheek against Kisses. Lucy Mae smiled at Kate over the top of Renee's head and gave her a broad wink.

Kate smiled back, warmed by the knowledge that

Lucy Mae had found more than one way of healing the wounds she had caused with her careless comments.

Another voice came over the loudspeaker, announcing that the Best in Show judging was about to commence.

Kate squeezed Renee's arm. "You'd better hurry. There may be another trophy coming your way."

Renee shook her head. "The first place in Kisses' class went to a Chihuahua from Hopewell. But I don't mind." Her eyes misted over, and she held up the trophy. "Having my Little Umpkins win this award means more to me than even a Best in Show could."

"I have to go make sure everything's in place," Lucy Mae said. "Why don't you come along and give me a hand, Renee?"

Renee nodded, and the two of them walked off together like the best of friends.

Lawton nodded to Kate and Paul. "Been nice talking to you. I guess I'd better go make the rounds and touch base with a few more of my constituents." He headed off to mingle with the crowd.

Paul slid his arm around Kate's waist. "Well, Katie girl, it's been quite a day."

"It has indeed." Kate started walking back toward the hospitality table, with Paul matching her steps. "I need to pack my things and put them away, then I think I'll be ready to go home and put my feet up for a while."

She took a long look around the park, from the bustle of activity at the show ring to the happy foursome climbing into Jeff Turner's truck.

"You know," she said, "I do believe the Hanlons can add another pastime to their résumés."

"In addition to your sleuthing skills?" Paul gave her one of his lopsided grins. "What's that?"

Kate looked up at him and laughed. "Isn't it obvious? Mysteries *and* matchmaking."

"True enough." Paul chuckled. "Since we're already a match made in heaven, how about solving a mystery for me?"

Kate tilted her head and gave him a puzzled look. "And what might that be?"

He leaned toward her and whispered in a dramatic tone, "The mystery of who gets the first taste of that ice-cream pie you've been hiding in the freezer . . ."

Kate bubbled with laughter. "That I can do, Pastor Paul. Mystery solved!"

About the Author

CAROL COX is the author of more than twenty novels and novellas. Her nonwriting time is devoted to being a pastor's wife, a homeschool mom and, recently, a grandmother. Carol makes her home with her husband and young daughter in northern Arizona, where the deer and the antelope really do play—often within view of the family's front porch. To learn more about Carol and her books, visit her Web site at www.CarolCoxBooks.com.

Mystery and the Minister's Wife

Through the Fire
by Diane Noble

A State of Grace
by Traci DePree

A Test of Faith
by Carol Cox

The Best Is Yet to Be
by Eve Fisher

Angels Undercover
by Diane Noble

Where There's a Will
by Beth Pattillo

Into the Wilderness
by Traci DePree

Dog Days
by Carol Cox